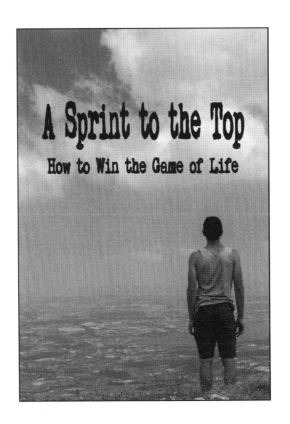

A Sprint to the Top

How to Win the Game of Life

Endorsements for *A Sprint to the Top*

"Dan Blanchard has his mind and heart on the struggles teenagers have to deal with. There are a lot of confusing issues out there, and he knows that it takes more than a dream to become a leader in your own life. It takes inner strength, and that's something teens are rarely being shown or taught in this day and age. In this book, Dan shares "what it takes" through an amazing story that draws you in and coaches you at the same time. I highly recommend his books to learn how to coach your teen through the ups and downs of life!"

Rick Titan, Transformational coach and speaker, a.k.a Razor Ramon—former professional wrestler, author of *Wrestling with Consciousness* and *Crush your Stress!*, creator of the Transformation Technique

"It has been a pleasure getting to know Dan Blanchard over the last few years. All readers out there should make it their mission to become more familiar with Dan and his teen leadership books, especially this second book, *A Sprint to the Top: How to Win the Game of Life*. This mysterious and inspiring teen leadership book will leave its readers in exciting anticipation of what they too can accomplish."

Jerry Labriola, former CT Senator, M.D., and author of the mystery novel, *Diamonds and Pirates*

"Dan Blanchard has done it again with another great teen leadership book. He really inspires teens, as well as all of us, to take that journey called life and make the best of it!"

Dr. Abraham Chamie, Ph.D., Retired educator and corporate manager, recipient of Lifetime of Service award from the Wrestling Hall of Fame

"Whether you're an athlete or not, you're going to like the simple insights for living a better life Dan Blanchard reveals in this book. Reading it will surely inspire you to become a better version of yourself, and to find ways to help others become better versions of themselves too. Well done, Dan!"

Robert E. Skelton, College and Olympic coach and wrestler, public school administrator

"Figuring out how to beat the odds is a challenge for many young men and women these days. It's not easy for them to ask for help, and sometimes it's even harder to find someone they trust enough to ask. Dakota comes face to face with the same kinds of issues many teens face, and through his experience, we see him work his way through all the twists and turns life deals him."

Shirzad Ahmadi - 13 World Wrestling Champion titles, 23 National Wrestling Champion titles, Military World Games wrestling gold medalist, only American to win 2 gold medals in 2 different styles of wrestling in Athens 2015 World Championship. 40+ years coaching high school and NCAA Division I, II, and III wrestlers, 38+ years as both a high school and college educator.

"Dan Blanchard has written another great motivational book that everyone should read!"

Sergeant Ernie Maynard, WWII and Korean War Veteran

"In his book *A Sprint to the Top,* Dan Blanchard has given us outstanding insight into the process of living life like a champion. Dan uses Dakota Kilmartin, his main character, to outline the steps one can use to live a successful life. Dakota attacks each day with tried-and-true techniques that have been employed by champions—and successful people everywhere—for years. Dan gets it. It's traveling through the "process" that makes for a championship life, not the outcome. He effectively rolls the competitive wrestling experiences that Dakota confronts into exciting passages that reflect the physical, mental, and emotional strains many teens face each day. I highly recommend this book for anyone looking to read an exciting story laced with valuable life-long wisdom and lessons."

Jim Day, Berlin High School wrestling coach, 2010 inductee into the National Wrestling Hall of Fame

"Reading this book will change your life for the better! Time after time Dan Blanchard and his message are inspiring teens, as well as all of us, to have faith in ourselves, faith in our place in this world, and faith in our journey of life-long learning."

Mary Jones, Former talk show host WDRC-AM

"Daniel Blanchard shares tons of ageless wisdom in his delightful book, *A Sprint to the Top: How to Win the Game of Life*. If you have a youngster, make sure to read it with them. Warning—you will most likely be surprised at how much important information you, yourself, will learn."

Rev. Trent Blanchard, M.A., HR Consultant, life coach, addiction specialist, radio talk show host, and author of *Triple A's for the Soul – Your Pathway to Personal Freedom*

"*A Sprint to the Top* offers keen insight into how, even at a very young age, anyone of us can use personal achievement, adversity, and even tragedy as motivation to reach the highest levels of success, and to have a profound effect on our futures, as well as, all those around us. Whether you're a wrestler, a student-athlete, or someone just trying to make it through today, you're going to like Dan Blanchard's story. Way to go Dan. Keep up all the good you're doing not only for our youth, but for all of us!"

Luke Lofthouse, Iowa Hawkeye All-American wrestler, Utah Valley wrestling assistant coach, former Iowa Hawkeye strength coach.

"Only Dan Blanchard could have written this powerful book of never giving up and willing ones' success. I've known Dan for many years, and this book is not just something filled with insight and success strategies that he wrote. It's how he's lived day in and day out while racking up one success and victory after another, under extremely difficult circumstances that would have caused others to stop short of what they are truly capable of. Everyone out there needs to read this book!"

John Knapp, Wrestling champion, founder and director of KT Kidz Wrestling, coach to over 100 state champions, 50 New England champions, 50 All-Americans, and 10 national champions.

"*A Sprint to the Top* continues the positive message from Dan's first book, *The Storm*: Valuable lessons that have been passed on to us by special people in our lives do not have to die if we continue to live thier lessons out in our lives. We honor them by allowing their light and wisdom to continue to shine through us. If you haven't read *A Sprint to the Top* yet, you need to!"

Betsey Katiti, Ugandan Princess

"Love it when I find another former athlete who is now using his energy and vigor to make the lives of our youth better through his inspirational teachings, books, and speeches! Keep up the good works you're doing Dan. You are making a difference!"

Danny Buggs, Former Washington Redskins wide receiver, author, and speaker

"Like Dan's first teen leadership book, *The Storm: How Young Men Become Good Men*, this sequel, *A Sprint to the Top: How to Win the Game of Life* should be required reading for every young man and woman in this country, as it teaches some valuable lessons that they might not hear anywhere else. Parents, get this book, read it, and then pass it on, as it needs to be read by as many young people—and the people who care for our young people—as possible."

Kathy DiCocco, Executive director of *The H.O.P.E. Foundation for a Better Tomorrow*

A Sprint to the Top

How to Win
the Game of Life

by

Dan Blanchard

Teen Leadership Publishing
Mansfield, CT

Edited by: Valerie Utton
Cover Design by: Valerie Utton

Published by: Teen Leadership Publishing
                  Mansfield, CT

Printed in the United States

Library of Congress: 2017913459

ISBN 10: 0-9862398-1-X
ISBN 13: 978-0-9862398-1-6

Other books by Dan Blanchard

The Storm: How Young Men Become Good Men

Granddaddy's Success and Social Skills Secrets for Kids:
How 30 Days and 150 Words can Improve Student
Performance and Social Emotional Learning

Evaluation of Professional Development
in an Urban High School: Includes
Specific Steps to Make PD Successful

x

Foreword

I met Dan through a mutual friend who insisted that I call him because he is an inner-city school teacher, coach, author, speaker, and former wrestling champion who is truly making a difference in the lives of our youth. I spoke to Dan on the phone, found him to be very genuine, and invited him to come out to Iowa to the United States Wrestling Olympic Trials so we could get to know each other better while watching some of the best wrestling in the world.

While at the Olympic Trials, Dan and I talked at length about the challenges young people are facing, most often with no real guidance or support. We agreed that things are tougher than ever and that too many adults are dropping the ball. With social media, it's easy for kids—and adults—to tune out of the struggles in their own lives and tune in to the lives and antics of celebrities, mini-celebrities, professional athletes, and reality stars. By default, they are today's easy access "role models." But call them out on their questionable behaviors and too many will rebuke that being a role model isn't part of their job.

We all need role models though, no matter how old we are. Without role models, we're more likely to shy away from choosing things that look too difficult or different. It just feels safer to take the easy route when there's not enough information about the choice in front of us, and there's no one around to offer guidance about a choice or a chance that could lead to something truly exciting. Dan and I were fortunate to have had both the chance and the choice to wrestle when we were young, and had the opportunity to build our character and become the men we are today because of this amazing and challenging sport.

There's no doubt that life can be hard for all of us sometimes, especially for those who are the most vulnerable. One of the best ways to keep moving forward in the face of life's adversities is to develop our own leadership skills, even if that just means leading our self. The simplest and easiest place to start is by reading about people who have faced struggle and adversity in their lives and still managed to find a better way.

This book is the sequel to Dan's first dynamic teen leadership book, *The Storm: How Young Men Become Good Men*, and picks up Dakota's journey after his day in the park with Granddaddy. Readers will discover things about themselves as they follow Dakota's journey forward, in spite of all that happens.

This book is a reminder of the important role each of us can choose to play in the life of another—no matter how old we are— by being a positive mentor and role model for someone else. And, for anyone with a competitive spirt, you're really going to love the second half of this book which takes place at an elite national-level wrestling tournament. But even if the only "wrestling" you're doing is with life, read this book and get ready to break free of whatever has you locked up in a tight straggling hold right now!

> Scott Schulte, New York Times Best Seller
> Author: *A Wrestling Life: The Inspiring Stories of Dan Gable*

Prologue

Journal entry, November 29

Tomorrow it will officially be a year since I've talked to Granddaddy. Tomorrow is my birthday too, well... our birthday... and all I can do is hope that he shows up again. A lot has changed and I really want to talk to him about it.

I got a social studies paper back from Mr. Evans today. On it he wrote, "You are a true aberration." I had to look up the word to find out if that was a good or bad thing. It means: a departure from what is normal, usual, or expected, typically one that is unwelcome. That didn't sound good, but I got an A+ on the paper so it can't be all that bad.

Maybe he wrote it because I'm a different person than I was last year. My outside is still the same. I still live in the same apartment, I'm still with Jenn, my family still hasn't changed, I still wrestle and play football, and I still deliver newspapers and work at the gas station. But the way I think about things on the inside has definitely changed.

And it's strange because it still feels like "me" on the inside, but now I think about things I never would have thought about before that day in the park with Granddaddy. Sometimes it's still hard to wrap my brain around everything I learned from him.

I remember that it took me weeks to write it all down, and even longer to look up the stuff I didn't understand.

Sometimes I wonder if the guys around me would have reacted the same way I did if they'd had a day like that. I don't know. I'm not really any different from them except that I think a lot. But everybody thinks. It's not like we can stop our brain from thinking. Maybe the difference with me is that I just think about different things.

I'd like to believe that people like Cristiano Ronaldo and LeBron James would have been considered aberrations when they were younger too. It's not that I think I'm like them, but I bet I have one thing in common with them. I think about what I want, and I don't let things get in the way. And when something does get in the way, I figure out how to get through it or around it.

I know what I want too. That's really important because if I don't know what I want, then how will I know if I'm moving in the right direction? So maybe knowing what I want, and doing what I have to do to get what I want is what makes me an aberration. Still don't know if I like the word, but if the result of being an aberration is being a success too, then I'm good with it.

"Do not let what you cannot do interfere with what you can do."

— *Coach John Wooden*

1.

After the Storm

"I'm not afraid of storms, for I am learning how to sail my ship."

— Louisa May Alcott

When the rain finally stopped, I stepped outside where the smell of the storm had quickly been replaced by the smell of clean fresh rejuvenating air. It was time to start my paper route, but I stopped long enough to take a deep breath and think about the fact that exactly one year ago today, Granddaddy and I had spent the afternoon in the park. My life had changed since the day he shared his secrets for living a great life with me. Before that afternoon, I'd believed I was doing okay. But after we talked, I felt like I was going to bust with all the amazing things he talked about. It had been too much for me to fully grasp in one sitting, but just as Granddaddy had promised, with each passing day more things made sense.

Sometimes remembering the way I used to think before that day makes me laugh. It had been my 16th birthday, and his 76th. Before talking to Granddaddy I actually believed that luck played a bigger role in my accomplishments than I did, and that luck would take over and get the job done when I couldn't. Maybe I thought that way because when it came to sports, people had a tendency to say things to me like "lucky break" when I did something no one expected me to be able to do. Now I understand that you don't need luck on your side to get things to turn out the way you want them to. And that what might look like luck to other people is more likely the result of hard work that's prepared us to take advantage of opportunities when they show up. I'd always been good at the hard work part, but I'd worked even harder over the last year and was feeling more confident than ever—like nothing could ever get in my way again.

I looked towards the early morning horizon and the beautiful rainbow shimmering into existence and smiled as another one of Granddaddy's secrets popped into my mind. He said that we should learn to appreciate life's "storms" because we all have storms in our lives. I'd already lived through a bunch of my own storms and knew there would be more. That was okay though, because storms produced rainbows too. I just needed to keep looking for them.

When I left Granddaddy last year, in that moment, I knew my life was going to be different. With each step I felt bigger, stronger, and more fortunate. When I turned back to thank him again, my mysterious Granddaddy was nowhere to be seen. He'd told me that even though I hadn't seen him, he'd been watching my progress while I was growing up and that he'd been at most of my wrestling matches and football games. He also said there were reasons why I never saw him, and reasons why it had to be that way. He didn't explain the reasons, but I didn't ask either. Considering how quickly he vanished that day, I just reckoned it was one of his many amazing skills.

Now it was a year later, and thanks to Granddaddy, I was more at peace with myself and the world around me. It was a good feeling, but there was something sad in it too because I hadn't seen him other than the few hours we'd spent together last year. What was I going to do if he didn't show up today? Or if I never saw him again? I had no idea. Either way, one thing was true... that day in the park had been one of the best days of my life! Since that day, I've tried my best to practice the secrets Granddaddy shared. For instance, I wasn't going to settle for just thinking I might be successful. I knew without a doubt I could be successful. I was going to live my life, doing all the things I told Granddaddy I would do, and be a success as a result.

When I got up this morning, I started my day the same way I start every day, visualizing my future success as if it were already a done deal. I'd been doing that for almost a year before my afternoon with Granddaddy, and for the most part, things were working out. Last year my wrestling team had a good year. We didn't place in the state championships like I'd visualized, but I placed as an individual. This year's football season just ended, and we did great, falling just one game short of the championship playoffs. Wrestling season was starting this coming Monday and I was already visualizing a successful season for both me and my team, while walking my morning newspaper route.

And even though I was only a junior, I'd already written down my goals for my senior year too: To win the state championships in both football and wrestling, to be the captain of both the football and wrestling teams, and to win the individual state wrestling title at the 145-pound weight class. The great part about knowing what my goals for next year are is that it makes it easier to figure out what I can do right now to set myself up for my future success. And thanks to Granddaddy's encouragement, I've started thinking about my success beyond high school too, which means thinking and planning my success beyond sports. I visualize opening my college acceptance letter and receiving my bachelor's diploma. I added getting better grades to my to-do list too. No more average grades for me! It's things like that that really make me feel like I'm taking charge of my destiny. And, I believe I can make it happen.

Granddaddy was the first person I ever told about how I wrote my goals down and visualized them as if they'd already actually happened. I was worried he would say that I was being too cocky, but he said that confidence was a necessary part of success, because without it, we wouldn't have the courage to reach for anything. "You've got to aim for something, so you might as well shoot for the stars. If you miss with the moon, you'll have accomplished more than most, you'll have a victory to celebrate, and you can still shoot for the stars."

He made me feel good about doing it too. He said that writing down my goals and thinking about them would make a tremendous difference in the long run. He told me to keep doing it, and I gave him my word that I would. We didn't talk about what giving my word meant that day, but it makes sense that if you give your word to someone and then don't keep it, it would be hard for that person, or anyone else, to trust or respect you. I was determined to be a man of my word because I wanted to have a solid reputation as a person who could be depended on to come through with what he said or promised.

Sometimes I wonder how much the way I think about things matters. There's a poster in one of our classrooms with the saying "Everything starts as a dream." It sounds true enough. If people didn't think about how to change things or make them better, we probably wouldn't have cars or computers because those things started out as dreams and ideas. I've heard a couple of famous people say that "thoughts become things" and that kind of makes sense too. If everything starts as a dream, well, a dream is a thought. If you keep thinking about it and how to make it happen, it's more likely to happen. Isn't that what Steve Jobs did with Apple? He had a dream about what a computer should be and didn't stop working on his dream until he was holding it in his hand.

Now when I look around, I don't just see stuff that's cool or useful. I can look at anything and know that it started out as a dream, idea, or thought in someone's head. Like most people, I've just gotten so used to having the things other people's dreams created around me that I wasn't thinking about what I might be able to do with my own dreams, ideas, and thoughts. I'm working on changing that by paying more attention to what I'm thinking about, but there are still plenty of times when my mind still wanders into the weird. At first I tried to figure out where those thoughts came from, but I gave up on that. What difference does knowing where they came from make? I'd rather focus on something I can actually control so that when I realize my thoughts are somewhere in outer space, I can regroup and refocus them in a better direction... because if my thoughts are going to become things, I'm going to do as much as I can to make sure they are good things!

One thing that really helped was figuring out that it's impossible to think two thoughts at the same time. For example, you can't think a negative thought and a positive thought at the same exact time. There isn't enough room for both of them in our brain—well at least not in my brain. At first I thought the goal was to not think any negative thoughts at all, but that was impossible. Instead, I got better at noticing when my thoughts were negative. When they were, I'd come up with something positive to think about instead. As soon as I shifted my focus onto a better thought, it pushed the negative thought right out of my mind.

I've been working on this for about six months now, and during that time I haven't come across one negative thought worth thinking about. They all lead to the same result too—living a life decided by someone else. I distinctly remember Granddaddy talking about the difference between living a life that's the result of the choices we deliberately make, and the default life society is always ready to provide when we accept the choices and decisions others are happy to make for us. As far as I'm concerned, there is only room for positivity in my brain because I'm going to live a life I chose.

It's like putting together links in a chain. I start by thinking about what I want. Then I figure out steps I can take to get me there. The steps are important because if I don't do anything, I'm not going anywhere no matter how much I want to. Pretty soon, the things I'm thinking and doing are all headed in the same direction. That means that if I think about something positive long enough, I'll eventually start acting in a way that's consistent with getting that positive thing. So I work hard on keeping my thoughts, actions, and behaviors in line with my goals, and am getting better at making decisions about which kinds of actions and behaviors will lead me to the future I want.

Over the past week I'd visualized meeting up with Granddaddy today about a million times. There were so many things I wanted to tell him about—like about all the reading I'd done since last November. At first I didn't think I was going to like it much, but this kind of reading was different. It wasn't like it was in school when I had to read about what happened to someone, or about what someone did. I was reading about real people, and about what really happened to them and around them. Most of them are long gone, but that didn't change the fact that at one time they were living, breathing and walking around just like I was right now.

Last week I read something General Patton of WWII said. "Fear kills more people than death. Death only kills once." If I hadn't spent that time in the park with Granddaddy, chances are very slim that I would have picked up that book and started reading it. But we did have our day in the park, and every day since, something I learned from him encourages me to think. That day in the park changed my life forever and I do my best to stay true to the lessons he shared. I thank God for that day, and for my Granddaddy.

2.

Granddaddy

"Seeing is not always believing."
— Martin Luther King Jr.

By the time I finished my paper route, the sky was clear of clouds. It was going to be a beautiful day, and I wondered if Granddaddy was going to take advantage of the weather and do a parachute jump. Last year, he jumped the day before our birthday so he could meet with me on our birthday. I smiled at the thought because I'd added a parachute jump to my list of things I was going to do, looking forward to the possibility of maybe even jumping with Granddaddy on a future birthday.

When I got home, I did what I usually did. I sat down with the morning paper to see what was happening around the world. I was distracted though and quickly flipped from one page to the next scanning the headlines when something caught my eye. It was a picture of me wearing a military uniform. It was a confusing picture because I'd never worn a military uniform. It definitely looked like me though. I looked at the top of the page and realized I was looking at the obituary column. Someone must have made a really bad mistake because I wasn't dead.

My breath caught when I saw the name under the picture. It wasn't a picture of me. It was a picture of Neil Kilmartin, Granddaddy, in his military uniform 60 years ago. My stomach turned and twisted into a tight knot. This couldn't be right. He

7

couldn't be dead. Surely someone would have told me if he had died. My eyes scanned the words below the picture, but I couldn't read them. They were just lines of print blurred by confusion and tears. I wiped my eyes and went back to staring at the picture.

In it, Granddaddy looked just like I did now, so he must have been somewhere between 16 and 17 years old. He'd told me that he lied about his age and enlisted in the Army-Air Force when he was sixteen. Was this a picture of him when he enlisted?

He hadn't told me how much we looked alike, and I'd never seen a picture of him when he was young. Was this why he'd talked to me? Was it because every time he looked at me he felt like he was looking into a mirror and seeing himself as a young man again?

Staring at the picture, made me feel even more connected to him. We'd had so much more in common than I'd realized, and I could feel the knowledge of this truth solidifying the invisible bond between us. He'd seen himself in me and watched me grow up without letting me see him, but he had been there for me all the same.

I was racked with emotion and heard my sobs echo in the empty room. I was the "tough guy" and I was crying, but I couldn't have stopped even if I'd wanted to. I cried for Granddaddy, and I cried for me. I cried for that special day we had together and I cried because we wouldn't ever have another day like that—not today, not ever. Most of all, I cried for all the lost time we could have spent together. That day in the park had been an incredible gift then, but now it was an irreplaceable treasure.

I thought of all the years Granddaddy said he'd been watching over me and was suddenly angry, mentally commanding him to come out into the open so I could talk about how well I'd been doing since we'd last met. But the anger was gone in a flash too. I just desperately wanted to see him once more—just once more so I could hug him and let him know how much he meant to me. I swiped away my tears with my shirt sleeve and took a deep breath, trying to find a way to be strong. I smoothed out the page in front of me and read.

Neil Kilmartin, 76, from East Hartford, CT, was a beloved man whose wisdom, brilliance, and wit touched those around him. He was born on November 30, 1925, in Hartford, CT, to the late Herbert and Mary Ann Kilmartin.

Neil joined the Army-Air Force after leaving high school at just 16 years old. An ace fighter pilot serving in the European theater during WWII, Neil shot down over 25 enemy aircraft. He was also a recipient of a Purple Heart.

After the war, he attended the University of Connecticut, receiving a B.S. in Political Science in 1949. Following graduation, he lived in Connecticut, spending the next 30 plus years working for the United States Government. During this time, he earned a Masters in International Relations from the University of Hartford, a Masters in Education Pedagogy from St. Joseph's College, and subsequently, two doctorates from the University of Connecticut in Political Science and World History.

He was an avid golfer and a member of a local golf club. He was also a devout Boston Red Sox and UConn Husky fan. Neil was a former president of the Boys Club. It was said that he loved the park and could often be found there, sitting at a picnic table admiring the flight of the birds. Neil was the youngest of six siblings and the last survivor of his family.

The ink on the page was smudged in a few places now. There was probably ink on my face too because I kept wiping tears away with ink-stained fingers. I glanced at the mirror hanging on the wall across the room and then back down at the paper. Looking at Granddaddy's picture was like looking into the mirror.

What was I supposed to do now? I looked around the room,

but no one else was home. Even if someone had been there, I'm not sure I could have talked. What would I say? I felt strange. It was like everything had changed, but at the exact same time like nothing had changed. I had really hoped Granddaddy was going to show up today, but if he hadn't it would have been okay because I always felt like he was there, in the wings, watching my back— always.

What was there to do now except get on with the business of the day? Is that what Granddaddy would want me to do? Is that what he would have done? I didn't know. The only thing I knew for sure in that moment was that my mission for today hadn't changed. It was still to live by the principles Granddaddy had shared with me last year so I could be more successful today than I was yesterday.

I'd spent every single day of the last year striving to live the principles he'd shared with me, and was proud of what I'd accomplished. He taught me about Kaizen and how important it was to focus on continuous self-improvement. He shared the secret of CANDI—constant and never-ending deliberate improvement—too. I'd imagined telling him about my accomplishments, and how he might put his hand on my shoulder and tell me how proud of me he was.

I wanted to tell him about all the times over the past year when something he'd shared with me had popped into my head out of nowhere. It was like my subconscious mind had been wrestling with Granddaddy's secrets and when it finally had one of them figured out, the gate to my conscious mind would suddenly open and I'd have an epiphany, or revelation, or whatever you want to call it. Something just clicked and I'd have a deeper understanding of what Granddaddy had been trying to convey to me. Like Buddha, I was becoming enlightened—exactly as Granddaddy had forecasted.

Sometimes when I had those aha moments, I got goosebumps, and all I could think was, "Wow." The past year had been filled with many moments like that, many moments of clarity and understanding. Just thinking about them had my head spinning, and I slammed my fist down on the table. This wasn't fair! I hadn't had enough time with him yet!

I looked down at Granddaddy's picture again and suddenly remembered him talking about how easy it was to waste time resenting and blaming people and situations from our past for our current circumstances. Was this one of those situations? Was I wasting time getting angry about something I couldn't control or change? And then I was having another aha moment, realizing that letting go of anger and resentments from the past didn't mean giving up everything from the past. Everyone's past included things worth carrying forward into the future. The challenge was making the distinction between what was better left in the past and what would be a benefit in the future.

I certainly had no intentions of giving up my wonderful memories of my day in the park with Granddaddy. Yes, I was going to have to face the fact that Granddaddy was gone now, and that we would never share another day in the park, but it would be unproductive to waste even one second carrying around feelings of anger and resentment for something I was powerless to change. Giving into negative thoughts and feelings wasn't going to make any of this easier to deal with either. They could however, definitely make things worse. Every minute I wasted on those negative feelings was a minute I could have spent thinking about all the good Granddaddy brought into my life.

That truth got me thinking about Pops too. I'd been working on "letting go" of my anger and resentment towards him during the past year, and it had worked to some degree, but my first reaction to him was still mostly anger and resentment. I tried to remind myself that people who hurt other people are usually hurting within themselves. But understanding that didn't mean what they did was okay. It was just that sometimes people did things because it was all they knew, and probably the result of what they saw and learned from other people while they were growing up. After they grew up, it was the only way they knew how to survive. Some people probably didn't even know there was a better way.

This past year I heard someone say, "People do the best they can do with the tools they have," and it got me thinking. I could look at Pops and say he did the best he could, but was that really true? If I can look at my life and decide I want to do better, doesn't that mean he could have made the same choice? I think it does, and that's probably why I still feel the way I do towards him. But I also think it's hard for people to change when they don't have anybody in their corner rooting for them to be a better person.

As soon as I realized I had Granddaddy in my corner, I made major leaps. I was on my own now though. Would I still be able to do it? Would I be able to keep up my forward momentum without Granddaddy? Or would I grow to resent him the same way Pops had grown to resent him for not being there when he was growing up?

I definitely didn't want that to happen. If I was going to fail, or fall short of my expectations, it wasn't going to happen because I didn't try. It wouldn't be because I limited myself by only working with the tools I had right now. I wanted to do the best I could for my future wife and children, and that meant staying focused on improving myself and what I had to offer. The only solution was to keep moving forward, even if it meant moving forward without Granddaddy in my life. What was the alternative? Going back to when I felt like I didn't deserve better?

3.

Our Past Does Not
Equal Our Future

"In the end, it's not the years in your life that count. It's the LIFE in your years."

— Abraham Lincoln

My mind was doing flip-flops. One second I was able to think about the good things Granddaddy brought into my life, but the next all I could think about was that I'd lost something I was never ever going to have again. I could feel that loser mentality threatening to creep into my mind too. It wasn't the same kind of feeling I got when I lost a football game or a wrestling match. It was more like the feeling that you're never going to have something because you're not good enough to have it.

When I was a kid, I didn't have reasons to feel good about myself, and I was convinced that no one else cared whether I lived or died. That's why I thought of myself as a loser. Then I found things to care about. At first it was just sports. Sure, I was angry when I started playing sports, but that changed, and football and wrestling had helped me build myself in more good ways than I could have ever imagined. I liked my jobs, and I liked working.

I had Jenn in my life too, and she was way better than sports or a job. Then Granddaddy stepped into my life and for the first time I felt like I had everything I needed to keep my momentum up. He was the last piece of the puzzle, but now he was gone and

13

so was his support.

Was there something I could have done that would have changed what happened? Would Granddaddy still be here if I had done something differently? I knew that was a crazy way to think. It wasn't doing me any favors either, so I searched my mind for something more positive to think about. *My past does not equal my future! Society and circumstances no longer control my life! My destiny is in my hands and mine alone! Our Creator does not create junk!* A line from one of blues singer L.C. Robinson's songs flashed into my mind too, "Things may happen around you, and things may happen to you, but the only things that really count are the things that happen in you."

My thoughts were still racing around inside my head, but I tried to calm my breathing as best as I could. My backpack was on the table to the left of the newspaper with a book by Booker T. Washington sitting on top of it. I picked the book up and opened it to a page I'd bookmarked. "I shall allow no man to belittle my soul by making me hate him." I'd put the bookmark there because I wanted to think about that when I had more time. It reminded me of what Granddaddy had said about running away from an over-bearing and cruel father, escaping into the military. He said that he'd forgiven his dad, and made a promise to himself to never again give anyone the power to make him hate.

I was trying to follow Granddaddy's example, and worked hard on forgiving Pops. I understood that the anger I felt towards Pops for the way he treated me had given him a lot of power over me. Forgiving him had released me from the hate. There were times when I could still feel the pull to hate him though, and right now was one of those times. If Pops had done a better job with his life, Granddaddy might have always been in my life.

Suddenly I realized Booker T's words might apply to me in a weird way too. Was I doubting myself so much that all my old thoughts would be able to gang up on me and get me to hate myself, and my life, like I did when I was a kid? I sighed because I knew it would never happen, but also because in that moment, I understood that I didn't need Granddaddy next to me to tell that anymore. I'd learned it on my own without him standing over my shoulder to make sure I didn't make that mistake. He'd showed me the entrance to a well-worn path and shared enough sage advice about how to continue the journey when he wasn't around.

I was just overwhelmingly disappointed that I wasn't going to be able to share how much I'd accomplished. There were so many things I wanted to talk to him about. I wanted to show him the new car I'd bought with money I'd put aside from delivering newspapers and working at the gas station. I could have spent more money and bought a better car, but I was following Granddaddy's example of living "a simple man's life," and decided to save my money instead. I even figured out how to invest some of it.

I'd picked this car because it had a CD player and a good sound system. Jenn and I listened to music, but we also listened to audio books. There was just something really inspiring about hearing someone speak the words. It was as if they were speaking directly to us. Pretty soon, we started calling it our "automobile university." The audio books all come from the library, so they didn't cost a penny and we got to listen and learn about things that were way beyond what we were learning in high school.

Buying the car really helped me understand what it felt like to shoot for the stars. It's good to aim for the abilities and incomes of the elite because we all need goals that are bigger than we are right now. Without them, we're more likely to stay stuck right where we are. My car might not have been brand new, but I was one of only three juniors who had been able to buy their own car. I knew plenty of kids in my class who had credit cards though. Most of them had already maxed out their cards though, and now had to take whatever job they could find to make their monthly payments. It seemed to me that if they continued that pattern, they'd end up with a life full of the kinds of stressors that put people into early graves. At the very least, they would struggle to live up to the full potential our Creator intended for each of us.

I could only hope that somehow Granddaddy knew how hard I was trying. I didn't make excuses, and I was succeeding. I wondered if he'd be surprised to know that I was trying to talk with everyone I met now. A year ago I was happy to listen to people tell me how good I was doing, but I never actually talked to them, and I never remembered their names. Just like Granddaddy had said though, I found some tricks for remembering people's names on the internet and now was pretty good at it. The more people I talked to, and the more books I read or listened to, the more convinced I was that I wasn't a loser condemned to a life of unhappiness due to conditions outside of my control. Again, my past does not equal my future!

All these great things were happening in my life and I was still a teenager! I felt good about the ways I was constantly preparing myself to be ready to meet opportunities when they were presented to me. I think that's how Granddaddy lived his life, and it was definitely how I wanted to live mine.

Granddaddy's obituary column was now drilling the "life in my years" philosophy into me every time I glanced at it. I wanted to remember the lesson, but I had to close the newspaper, new tears letting me know how much I wanted myself and everyone around me, even my Dad, to have that life in their years. It made me sad to know that I couldn't do anything about what other people chose to do—or not to do—when it came to how they were going to live their lives. Maybe one of the reasons people don't live their lives to the fullest is because they forget that living isn't something you do one day and then you do something else tomorrow. Living is something we get to do every day. It's a choice we get to make every day when we wake up.

Our Past Does Not Equal Our Future

There were always be days when it was definitely trickier than others, but Dr. Steven Covey wrote this thing about "sharpening the saw" and how the tools we use to live our lives can become dull when we use them over and over again without any thought to how well they're working. When we do that, life becomes dull too. There are also times when things just don't go the way we wanted. Now when I have one of those days, I consider it a reminder to think about ways I can sharpen my tools and efforts.

I bet even Granddaddy would have been impressed to hear me say that.

A Sprint to the Top

4.

Living Large

"Let us live so that when we come to die even the undertaker will be sorry."

— Mark Twain

In a year-and-a-half, I was going to graduate from high school and be out on my own. My plan was to always be fully awake and aware of the choices I was making, and to continue pushing the limits of what was possible for me. Doing that would put me in the position of being able to grow and improve my life, and hopefully, the lives of others, for the better. I just never imagined I'd be doing it without Granddaddy. He was like a security protocol that would kick in if something went wrong... except that instead of alarms going off, he would suddenly appear if I was headed in the wrong direction. There had been plenty of storms in my life over this past year, but gratefully, he never showed up and my confidence continued to grow. After all, if he didn't show up, that meant he thought I was doing okay.

I wasn't feeling very grateful right now though. There still so many questions I wanted to ask him—like about death. Everything we'd talked about last year was about life, and what we could do to make sure we lived a purposeful, meaningful, and passion-filled life. The closest we got to the subject of death was talking about not letting opportunities for living pass us by.

The truly weird part was that I couldn't seem to wrap my brain around the fact that he was gone. Even now I felt like he was still watching out for me; but was that even possible? At one point during our conversation last year he'd said that there were reasons why he wasn't around, and why he never stepped out of the crowd. He'd even gone so far as to say that it was safer if I didn't know. So in my gut, I always felt like he was there, even when I didn't see him. That knowledge hadn't stopped me from looking for him though, and over the last year, I'd looked through the crowds at wrestling matches and football games, always hoping to catch a glimpse of him. I never did, but I never doubted he was keeping tabs on me either. Sometimes it was like I could hear his voice inside my head guiding me, his words acting like a compass when I was trying to understand something or make a decision. There were times when I said something to someone and realized I even sounded like him.

Wouldn't I know it in my gut if Granddaddy was really... gone? It was hard to even think the word "dead," and now my head was starting to fill with impossible ideas about the difference between being "gone" and being "dead." I opened the newspaper back to the obituary and read it again. This time something jumped out at me. It didn't say when or how he died. I checked all the other obituaries, and sure enough, most of them said something about how the person died. Was it possible that this was Granddaddy's way of letting me know that he wasn't really gone?

That was a crazy thought. How could anybody pull something like that off? It would be a crazy thing to do, and I'd be crazy to think it was true. Nuts to think Granddaddy would be speaking to me through an obituary column. And even if he could pull that off, why would he do it? Why wouldn't he just show up today on my 17th birthday like he did last year on my 16th birthday?

Showing up was what a normal person would do, right? If he was alive, he could just step out of whatever crowd he'd concealed himself in, let me know he was okay, and then go back to that place he goes to—wherever that is—when he isn't around. On the other hand, normal people don't jump out of airplanes when they're 76 years old.

I felt my face getting red, my skin getting hot, and my hands getting clammy. This was crazy! I couldn't believe I was even entertaining the ludicrous idea that Granddaddy could still be alive. His picture was right in front of me. His obituary was right in front of me. Even though it could have been a picture of me, it wasn't. It was Granddaddy, plain as day, in black and white.

There was a part of my brain trying to convince me to accept the printed truth so I could start the process of moving on with my life. Granddaddy had impressed upon me how powerful moving forward was, and that's what I needed to do right now... accept the situation and move forward. At the very least, I owed him that.

I stood and tried to think about the day ahead. It was a Saturday, and I'd been so sure that Granddaddy was going to show up that I'd already planned on spending the day with him. Now it was like my brain was doing flip-flops. One second I was trying to wrap it around the fact that Granddaddy was dead, but in the next I couldn't seem to force myself to travel down the road to accepting his death. The logical thing was to accept it. But wouldn't it also be logical that someone would have told me he died before I had to read it in the newspaper?

I sat back down, again, and read through the other obituaries, comparing them to Granddaddy's. Sure enough, all those people had passed away at least three days before the obituary was printed. That was the way things were done—ordinarily. But then Granddaddy was no ordinary guy in life, so why would he be an ordinary guy in death?

And then that crazy thought popped into my head again—was it possible that Granddaddy wasn't dead? If there was one thing I learned from him, and all the people I've been reading and learning about since, it was that blindly accepting what you see and hear as truth can be a dangerous thing to do. If you have questions, ask them. When you aren't sure, investigate the situation so you can make your own informed decision about what's really going on.

If Granddaddy was really dead, then I'd have to believe it was just a coincidence that he died three days ago so that his obituary would be in today's paper, on our birthday. That was tough to believe. Surely my mom would have known if he'd passed away and told me before I had to read it in the newspaper. On the other hand, if by some miracle he wasn't dead, then the obituary could have been Granddaddy's way of letting me know he wasn't coming today. Granted, that was a stretch, but Granddaddy knew I got up early everyday to deliver newspapers. He also knew that I would be looking through the newspaper to keep myself informed about what was going on in the world. He had to know there was no way I was going to miss a picture that looked like me. He had to know I'd see it.

I looked at the other pictures on the page and sure enough, his was the only "young" picture. I dragged my hands down my face and smiled in spite of myself. It would be like Granddaddy to leave me a mystery to solve—something that would force me to think, ask questions, come up with a plan, and then take action. I nodded my head understanding the risk of taking on the challenge too. At the end, I would know if he was alive or dead. Could I do it? Was I up to the challenge?

Over the past year, I'd had the same dream a few times. In it, I'm standing in front of a large group of people. I have something really important to tell them, but when I open my mouth to speak there aren't any words in my head. The crowd gets restless, but I'm frozen to the spot, my mouth opening and closing like a fish. Now the crowd gets louder and starts laughing at me. I want to run away, but I can't. Suddenly, Granddaddy's standing behind me. He puts his hand on my shoulder and calmly and quietly whispers to me that fear tries to trick us into believing that we can't have a better future, so we should just forget about the future and take the easier road of just taking care of ourselves. As I listen to him, the fear in me drifts away and I'm now able to talk to the audience. I talk about all kinds of different things in those dreams, but the topics are always about something Granddaddy shared with me, that I want to share with them.

After doing some reading about dreams, I figured out that this was a fear dream. When I'm awake, I generally don't have a problem getting through times when I'm afraid. It comes down to really looking around and figuring out the difference between what I can and can't do. As soon as I figure that out, I take action by doing what I can do. What would be the point of trying to do what I can't do? But in my dreams, it's not always easy to see the difference. So now when I wake up after one of those dreams I start thinking about what's going on in my life that might be bothering me without me realizing it.

I've learned that fear can be sneaky, and that there are different kinds of fear. There's the kind of fear you get when you hear tires screeching because someone's slammed on their car's brakes. The sound makes you pay attention so you can avoid getting hit by a car. That's a legitimate fear. But there are other kinds of fear too. I read that the word FEAR stands for "False Evidence Appearing Real." I think that's what those dreams were about. They were my brain's way of trying to keep me from taking risks.

I knew there was a risk with investigating Granddaddy's death, and the thought of it was pretty scary, but I think the risk was mine—not Granddaddy's. If my prayers were answered, I'd find out he was alive. If they weren't answered... well... then I'd have to deal with that too. Either way, I'd have an answer at the end.

A Sprint to the Top

5.

The Journey Begins

"Sometimes it's the journey that teaches you a lot about your destination."

— Drake

My decision made, the first thing I wondered was if I was capable of investigating something like Granddaddy's "alleged" death. I believed I was. Over the past year I'd gotten used to looking deeper into things—like when I had a question about something I was thinking about. I wrote a lot of those questions down in the journal Granddaddy gave me so I wouldn't forget them. Some questions were easier than others to answer, but some were big questions, bigger than I could answer yet.

Reading books helped. When I read, I found answers to some of my questions, but I also found answers to questions I didn't even know I had. I wrote about what I was learning too. I'd already filled the journal Granddaddy gave me, and was about halfway through another. The nice thing about writing in my journal was that it helped me contemplate my own thinking. I couldn't write as fast as my mind was thinking, so when I wrote things down, my mind stayed more focused and I ended up doing a better job of figuring things out. I read somewhere that psychologists call "thinking about your own thinking" meta-cognition, and it's supposedly a "higher order" thinking—whatever that means.

All I knew was that pondering my own thinking worked. Now

when I was trying to figure something out, I started by writing it all down so I could get a good look at it. I asked myself questions too. Fortunately, finding answers to my questions wasn't like answering questions on a test in school. School questions were always other people's questions, and 99% of the time there was only one right answer (at least as far as the person who came up with the question was concerned).

Asking questions and writing down all the possible answers helped me understand what Granddaddy meant when he said that our Creator never gave us more than we could handle. As soon as I started writing things out, they hardly ever looked as bad as they did at first. It was like plotting a course on a map, with me trying to figure out how to get from point A to point B. The easy part was identifying point B. Point B was the result I was visualizing in my mind. The harder part was figuring out where point A was.

To plot a successful course towards any goal, I needed clear goal-oriented thinking. On the surface, it would be easy to think that point A would be right where I was standing, but that wasn't always the case. Sometimes my true point A was hidden behind or beneath other stuff. Right now, my point A was buried underneath all the emotions swirling around in my mind. If I let them, those emotions would definitely cloud my ability to figure out the point A of Granddaddy's disappearance. With practice, I'd gotten pretty good at figuring out point A's, realizing that most times it wasn't really any harder than taking care of simple things, such as making sure there was enough gas in the tank before heading out. If I was in too much of a hurry though, or my mind was too full of racing thoughts and emotions, I tended to be so focused on point B that it was hard to think or see anything else. Point A was like the starting point a GPS system needed before it could plot a course to point B.

Thinking about my point A's was a habit now, and I'd gotten better at asking the kinds of questions that helped me define my starting points. Somewhere along the way I read a quote that said, "If you don't like the answer you're getting, ask a different question!" After reading that, I noticed that some of the questions I was asking were just too big to answer, more like how to get from point A to point Z questions, than point A to point B questions. As soon as I started breaking all those bigger questions down into smaller ones, it started getting easier to plan things out.

A couple of weeks into football season, my coach told me that "I was coming into my own." I had to do a little internet research to find out exactly what that phrase meant, and was relieved to find out it was a good thing. It meant I was standing on my own two feet, my confidence was growing, and I was developing my own voice. I had to agree. Being willing to ask questions—even when they were tough to ask—had helped me face adversity with more confidence and success than ever.

The physical challenge I was facing right now was that I didn't really have anything to start my investigation with other than a gut feeling that Granddaddy wasn't dead. The mental and emotional challenge I was facing was all about the fear that he really was dead, and that no amount of investigating was going to change that. My mind and heart were both racing again as a result of that fear, and it took many deep breaths for me to settle into a place where I could think clearly.

It was a fact that my gut was usually right, so maybe my gut had caught something that my conscious mind had missed because it was too busy trying to manage all my emotions. Again, I looked down at the obituary and started reading. After the first three sentences, I paused. Usually when I read the paper I heard my own voice in my head. But this time, I was hearing Granddaddy's voice. I read the lines again, and sure enough, they didn't read as if some staff writer had written them. They sounded like Granddaddy, so I slowed down and read each line carefully.

Nothing I read sounded like a clue, but I did find something that was incorrect. It said that Granddaddy was the last survivor of his family. I knew that wasn't true because Pops was still alive. Other than that, I didn't know enough about Granddaddy to know if some of the other stuff was true or not... except for the part about him liking to spend time in the park admiring the flight of the birds. I clearly remember him saying how watching birds in flight was a good reminder of how important it is to take the time to appreciate simple things rather than to take them for granted. This whole year, I'd made sure to carve out time to stop and appreciate all the good things in my life. There were still things that weren't perfect and needed more work, but for the most part, my life was definitely better than it was last year. My relationships were better because I'd taken the time to appreciate them too. Things were still complicated with Pops, but that was a whole other subject.

I sighed and rubbed my eyes. If things had gone the way they should have gone today, Granddaddy and I would have gone back to that park, sat, talked, and watched the flight of the birds together. Wait... maybe that was it! Maybe that was the clue he'd left for me. I was reading this on a day when we would have gone to the park, and it said right in the obituary that he could be found sitting there. It might be more coincidence than clue, but it was definitely the type of clue I think Granddaddy would leave.

Now I had a place to start, the same red picnic table Granddaddy and I sat on last year. As I grabbed my car keys, I wondered if Granddaddy knew I had the day off. He probably did. It was Saturday and I'd already finished delivering papers, so the rest of the day was clear. Maybe that was part of his plan... to give me a puzzle to solve on a day I'd have time to work on it. I was almost feeling excited, but I was nervous too. I didn't know what I was going to find when I got to the park, and suddenly, I didn't want to go alone. Gratefully, I knew I didn't have to. Jenn had the day off too, so I texted her and filled her in.

I sat in the car outside her house waiting for her to come out, the newspaper in my hand. We had both hoped she would get to meet Granddaddy today, but now I wasn't sure what was going to happen. When she climbed in, she leaned over and hugged me. "Are you alright?"

I shrugged. I knew I could trust Jenn with anything, but there was no way I was going to let my emotions take over right now. I had a mission, and a destination, so I pulled away from the curb and focused on the road and my driving.

We didn't talk during our ride to the park, but that's one of the things I love about Jenn. She wasn't one of those girls who always needed to be talking, or asking me if something was wrong when I didn't have anything to say. When we were together, we didn't always have to be talking or doing something. Sometimes it was enough just to be together. She always listened to me when I talked though, and I'd talked plenty over the past year about the things Granddaddy had said, or about things I'd read about.

She was the only person besides Granddaddy I'd ever told about my long-term goals and about how I'd written a mission statement. She'd seen how much my work ethic had improved since my 16th birthday, and witnessed how much my self-confidence and willingness to persevere had grown. She knew how much my goal of earning a high placement in this year's state-wrestling tournament meant to me too. Heck, if a few things went my way, once the dust of the championship rumble settled I could be standing on the top block of the winner's podium as the new CT state champion!

Jenn had seen how much I'd improved over the past year and decided to invest in her future too. She was on the girl's basketball team and had started working harder off the court, expecting the extra work to pay big dividends for both her and her team. Basketball was a team sport though, so we talked about the fact that one person can't take on all the responsibility for a good or bad season. On the other hand, one person's confidence can definitely have a positive impact.

I'd seen the effects of that firsthand during this past football season. My coach was a good motivator, and I listened to every word he said to us before games and during half-time. There were a couple of games when I saw teammates who were down because of the way things were going, or whose heads just weren't in the game, get psyched to pick up their level of effort after listening to what he said. I had listened to Granddaddy's words and they had made a huge difference in my life. It made sense. Sometimes, we can raise each other up.

It was nice knowing that Jenn and I shared the same kinds of goals. In one of the books I read it talked about yin and yang, and that was how I thought about the two of us... how well we worked together and how we complimented each other. We "spotted" for each other in the gym, and I was really glad she was with me because today, she was "spotting" for me for sure. She always had my back.

The closer we got to the park, the more my stomach turned. I wanted to get to the picnic table and see Granddaddy sitting there with a big smile on his face, proud of me for discovering and solving his puzzle. I wanted to introduce my two favorite people in the whole world to each other. If Granddaddy wasn't there, I had no idea what I was going to do.

I drove through the entrance to the park and headed towards the parking lot closest to the pavilion we'd sat in last year. It was impossible to see through the trees to the pavilion, and when I parked the car, I hesitated. Jenn took my hand and gave it a squeeze. I returned the squeeze and turned off the engine, ready for whatever was going to happen next.

6.

The Old Tattered Red Picnic Table

"Life is like art. You have to work hard to keep it simple and still have meaning."

— Charles de Lint

My heart was racing as Jenn and I quickly walked towards the pavilion. I could see the tattered red picnic table and knew it was the same one Granddaddy and I'd sat on. Just seeing it brought that day back to life in my mind. But that was all it brought. Granddaddy wasn't there. We stood by the table and looked around, but there was no sign of him... no evidence that he'd been there, and no obvious clue sticking out like a sore thumb.

I sat in the exact same spot I'd sat last year, patting the table next to me. Jenn sat, and we held hands, taking in the pavilion and the park around us. I remembered what Granddaddy had said about recalling things. You do it by trying to recreate the same conditions you'd experienced the first time around.

For example, if you were cold when you learned something the first time, then being cold again would help you remember what you'd learned. If you were tired when you learned something, waiting until you were tired again would make it easier to get yourself in the right state of mind to remember something you forgot.

I'd tested this idea last spring—getting myself back into the same state of mind as when something originally happened—and figured out that I could study smarter by making sure I was in the right state of mind when I studied. The first thing I tried was only studying when I wasn't tired. I was never tired when I took a test, so I didn't want to be tired when I studied for a test. It worked. I still had to study, but for some reason it didn't feel like the same amount of work. And it was a lot easier to remember what I studied when I was taking the test. My grades had definitely improved... one more thing Granddaddy helped me with.

It wasn't supposed to rain today anymore, but it was still November 30th, and there was definitely a chill in the air. I closed my eyes and concentrated on my environment. I could feel the nip in the air, the table beneath me, and hear the sounds of the park around me. I slowly inhaled until my lungs were filled and felt a smile taking hold of my face, remembering Granddaddy drawing in a deep breath and proclaiming that he could "smell the coming of rain." I'd thought he was kidding, but followed his example and took in a deep breath of my own. I hadn't smelled anything, but he was right about the rain. It turned into a storm I'll never forget!

It wasn't like I doubted him or didn't believe him when he said it, but before I went to bed that night I went online to see if someone could really smell something like rain. Turns out they can. I found out that our sense of smell is one of the most powerful memory triggers we have. There was even a quote by Russian-born American novelist Vladimir Nabokov: "Nothing revives the past so completely as a smell that was once associated with it."

Everything about our ability to smell is weird. Like the fact that we don't have labels for smells the same way we do for things like colors and sounds. We can look at a cloudless sky and label the color "sky blue." We can listen to music and label it as rock, country, hip-hop, or whatever too. On the other hand, smells can't be seen or heard, so we can't label them the same way. When we smell something our brain can't identify, we start looking around for the source of the smell. If someone starts telling a story about a stinky wet dog, anyone who's had a close encounter with a stinky wet dog knows how bad of a smell it can be. We all know what peanut butter smells like too. But if we didn't have those objects around for us to connect the smell with, how would we ever explain them? How could anyone ever explain what a wet dog smelled like to someone who'd never smelled one before?

I might not have been as good as Granddaddy was at identifying rain, but I could definitely smell snow before it snowed. Right now, the smell of the cool brisk autumn air carried the scent of fallen leaves, reminding me of the football play-offs and the semi-final game we'd played and lost a week ago. It had been an emotional rollercoaster, and sitting here now, breathing in the air with my eyes closed, I could just about hear the crowd's cheers, moans, and groans.

I noticed other things too. Jenn shifted her weight and I caught the sweet scent of her perfume. I loved the smell of her perfume. It reminded me of her and of how good being with her made me feel. I was very aware of the fact that my butt was getting numb from sitting on the hard picnic table too—just like it had last year. My nose was cold, and I could feel the cold on my cheeks. The more I gave into the sensations of what was around me, the easier it was to travel back into the state of mind that had captured me for a whole afternoon last year.

I let my mind fill with gratitude for Granddaddy, and could almost sense him getting ready to share more of his wisdom. With my eyes still closed, my breathing deep and even, I willed myself to be open. I heard something, and goose bumps covered my arms. The sound was very faint at first, but grew louder as it came closer. I listened intently and was certain I was hearing the wings of a bird in flight. I opened my eyes and instantly caught sight of the large bird circling in the sky just beyond the pavilion. Jenn and I both jumped off the table and stepped to the edge of the pavilion to get a better look. It was a bald eagle, and it soared in graceful arcs overhead.

We just stared in awe for a while, and I was happy to recognize how easy it was for me to appreciate what I was seeing. Last year, I wouldn't have given it a second thought. But this year, I understood what a great gift this was. How could anyone not appreciate seeing something as elegant as this bird in flight? More of Granddaddy's words came back to me. "Don't ever let your life get so complicated that you end up negotiating it away for things that don't matter. Never forget the miracle you truly are, or all the miracles you're surrounded by every day. When you take the time to really look at the world, you'll begin to see all the possibilities."

I hadn't found any evidence that Granddaddy was still alive yet, but seeing the eagle reminded me that the clue in his obituary had led me to this park and to the experience of seeing this bird in flight. And in that moment, I felt like I was exactly where I was supposed to be. I was ready for my next message or clue now too, but had no idea where to look for it or what to do to find it.

Jenn must have seen my expression change and leaned into my shoulder. I put my arm around her, thinking of Granddaddy telling me how his wife completed him, and how he would have never achieved the level of success he had without her. I was so glad Jenn was with me. Together, I knew we could figure out the mystery Granddaddy had dropped into my lap via the morning paper. We watched the eagle until it flew out of sight, and then went back to the picnic table, both of us lost in our own thoughts.

Had my life really changed so much in just a year? Well, maybe not my outer circumstances. I still lived at home, and dealing with Pops was still a struggle, but my inner world had sure changed. Granddaddy had said it would. He explained that once I understood the information he was sharing, I could never unknow it, and that my new understanding would help me make better choices and decisions. Before that day, I really believed that God hated me, or at least didn't care anything about me. I didn't feel like that at all now. The weird part was that it wasn't like God changed me or my situation. I think I did most of the changing on my own. And now I felt like God smiled when I made a choice, a decision, or a change that had me moving in a good direction. Even when I made a mistake—and I definitely still made them—it was like he was smiling because at least I was trying.

I definitely didn't sit around hoping to "get lucky" anymore. I didn't sit around waiting for the brass ring to drop into my lap either. Instead, I kept my eyes open looking for little changes that could make my days better while cutting out things that made my days less productive. Last spring, I decided I wanted to get up earlier and tried getting up an hour earlier every day. I couldn't manage it. I got tired too early at night and was cranky most of the time, so I stopped trying. Then one day I was in the weight room and it was time to increase the weight on one of the machines. I moved the pin up five pounds and something in my head clicked. Maybe getting up earlier would work if I did it in increments instead of trying to do it all at once. So I tried setting my alarm clock for five minutes earlier. It was a "start small and keep building" strategy that worked like a charm.

Five minutes might not have been much, but it was enough to get me moving in the right direction. As soon as my body adjusted to the first five minute increment, I set the alarm another five minutes earlier. As soon as it was easy to get up ten minutes earlier, I added another five minutes. Now I was getting up a total of 35 minutes earlier than I used to. I really liked having that extra time too. It was quiet and I could use it to read or study or do whatever. But the best thing about that time was that I felt like I created it. It didn't really exist for me until I recognized it was possible, and then did what I had to do to turn the potential of more time into a reality. I wasn't sure if all of life was a do-it-yourself project like this, but my life certainly felt like it was full of a lot more potential.

There's definitely something to be said for making things happen over waiting for them to happen. I didn't want my life to be determined by other people's social, cultural, or political priorities and opinions about what I could or couldn't do. I was my own person, and not only did I have the right to choose the kind of person I wanted to be—just like everyone else—I also had the right to travel down the path I believed would get me there.

My friends and classmates on the other hand, seemed to be oblivious to the opportunities around them. I didn't know how they could miss the ones right in front of their faces, but they did. And yet each one of them had the ability to do better than they were currently doing. Instead, they just seemed to be content with doing the minimum required to get by. Granddaddy had nailed the result of that choice too. Minimum effort produced minimum results.

When I started expecting more out of myself, it didn't take long to realize that most people don't even try. And sometimes my decision to put more effort into what I was doing left me feeling like I didn't fit in. There just seemed to be this huge middle ground where there was a lot of pressure to walk in the same direction, at the same pace, as everybody else. A year ago I didn't understand that. Now when I looked around at my friends and classmates it was easy to guess who was going to end up living their life by default. I didn't know if I was going to do better than them or not, and realizing that really scared me at first. It felt like a tremendous weight—being responsible for how and where I would end up. It still scares me sometimes. But then I remember how bad my life was a year ago. So much had changed, all because of the things I was doing now. So even if I did screw up, all I had to do was stop long enough to figure out what the next best thing to do was. Good things can happen when preparation meets with opportunity... very good things.

My life was pretty exciting now because of all this... vision? Is that what Granddaddy would have called it? Opportunity? Action? Most of the time, it felt like a combination of all three. I still had my vision board. I'd gotten much better at looking for and recognizing opportunities too—especially when I was wrestling. My focus was better, and I wasn't just waiting around for the other guy to make a mistake. Instead, I was always on the lookout for an opening to make the move that would finish it. There was something about thinking this way that changed things. I knew that my hard work and persistence were going to pay off. For one thing, there were very few people my age who thought about where their lives were headed for more than a few weeks or months at a time. Very few had a plan, were willing to work hard, or had the mental toughness to stick to their guns when times got tough. It was easy to make excuses. Easier still to give up and join the other middle-of-the-road students who will grow up to be middle-of-the-road people content to blame anyone and everyone else for how their lives turned out.

Part of me wished I could help them. I'd have been happy to share everything Granddaddy shared with me, but I didn't get the feeling anyone was interested in hearing what I had to say. I came across a Buddhist proverb one day that put the situation into perspective for me. "When the student is ready, the teacher will appear." Maybe that explains what happened to me. Maybe I was ready and Granddaddy appeared. And even though I hadn't talked to him or seen him since, I found a lot of other great teachers in books, movies, and on the internet. Granddaddy was an awesome teacher, but if someone didn't have a granddaddy, or a dad to talk too, there were still plenty of opportunities and possibilities out there.

I walked back to the picnic table and brushed my hand across some of the messages that had been carved into it. Jenn followed my gaze and we both started reading. There were a lot of hearts with initials carved in them. A few R.I.P.'s too. Jenn began to read some of the "lovebird" declarations out loud.

"Manny loves Kiana... Jessica and Jonathan forever... Donovan heart Emily... "Jenn and Dan," she said giggling softly.

Then silence.... Then more silence.... "That one's weird," she said. "It doesn't really fit in with the rest."

"What does it say?" I asked, leaning forward to get a better look.

Jenn's brows furrowed as she spoke the words grooved inside a carved box. "Live a simple man's life."

I stared at the carving she pointed out for a while. "I've got it!" I announced, turning and heading towards the parking lot.

"You've got what?" she asked matching my pace as I started running towards the parking lot.

"The clue I was looking for."

"Where was it?"

I opened the car door for her and she got in. I ran around the car, climbed in, and started it up. "That carving you read to me. That was the clue."

She shook her head. "I don't get it. Where are we going?"

"We're going to a simple man's house!"

7.

A Simple Man's Home

*"I have come back again to where I belong; not
an enchanted place, but the walls are strong."*

— Dorothy Rath

We were cruising down the beautiful country road until the low stone wall on the left side of the road came into view. As soon as I saw it, I eased up on the gas pedal, letting the car slow down on its own.

"Are we there?" Jenn asked.

I nodded. Jenn didn't recognize where we were because she'd never been here before. Nor did she have any idea of how many times I'd driven down this road on my own. It wasn't because I was trying to keep it a secret. It was more about the fact that Granddaddy hadn't ever told me where he lived.

At first, I thought his address might be a secret no one was supposed to know, but I found it in an old address book we had at home. I checked online too, and sure enough, there it was. The problem was that if it wasn't a secret, then why hadn't he said something like, "I hope you'll stop by someday" or "The next time we meet we can do it at my house."

The beautiful man-made stonewall was set back a few feet from the road's edge. It was tall enough to block the view from the ground up to where the green foliage of maple and oak trees took over, tall sentinels blocking the rest of the view from the road. Those trees were bare now, revealing the strategically placed spruce and cedar trees that blocked the view at this time of the year.

I knew from experience that the driveway was coming up on the left and let the car slow to a crawl, remembering the first time I turned into Granddaddy's driveway. I'd stopped as soon as I'd made the turn, unable to muster up the courage to drive any further. Instead, I sat there for about a minute, chickened out, backed out, and went home. After a few days, I decided that Granddaddy had never actually told me I couldn't visit him. In fact, he told me that I should reach for the things I wanted, and I wanted to visit him, so I went to his house again.

I tried a bunch of times over the past year, each time visualizing Granddaddy answering the door and inviting me in. But no one ever answered the doorbell or my knock. If I'd had a phone number for him I could have called him and asked him if I could come over, but I didn't have his number. There wasn't a phone number listed in the address book at home. I asked my mom if she had his number, but she didn't. I called information and even tried looking it up online, but never found it.

The house always looked lived in though. There were potted plants on the porch and plants surrounding the house that always looked perfect. The lawn was always mowed too, and it was easy to imagine Granddaddy taking the time to do the work himself. For whatever reason though, no one had ever been home when I stopped by.

I always wondered where he was though. Was he off doing something exciting? I even asked my dad if he knew where Granddaddy went when he wasn't around. He'd rolled his eyes and answered in a voice full of sarcasm.

"He's off somewhere being Mr. Successful and saving the world again."

After that, I decided not to ask Pops or Mom anymore questions about Granddaddy. It was hard to imagine that

Granddaddy knew he was going to be off "saving the world" last year... unless meeting with me had been part of his plan all along. I tried to deny how that thought made me feel, but it burned inside of me all the same. He could have trusted me, and then we could have spent more time together before he left. If it turned out that he really was dead, then I'd go back to being that kid who didn't have anyone in his corner all over again. I had Jenn, and she meant the world to me, but Granddaddy was a man, and no matter how anyone tries to dissect it, boys need men to look up to.

My hands had a white-knuckle grip on the steering wheel, and my heart was pounding so hard I was sure Jenn could hear it. I almost jumped when she touched my hand.

"Are you going to turn in?" she asked.

I looked and realized I'd turned on the blinker and stopped the car, but hadn't made the turn. I took a deep breath, made the turn and drove around the bend in the driveway past a row of cedar trees.

Jenn sucked in a breath. "Wow," she said. "Nice."

I nodded in agreement as the grounds and house came into full view. Granddaddy's property, with all its natural beauty, was big. But it was also very private. In the same way that you couldn't see the house from the road, you couldn't see the road, the neighbors, the telephone wires, or anything else once you were inside the stone wall. If I hadn't driven here before, I wouldn't have had a clue that there were neighbors on both sides. There was just so much land and so many trees between the properties that you couldn't see or hear them. We could hear the birds though, and for a moment, I felt at peace and reassured that I was right where I was supposed to be.

I was always amazed when I came here. Each time it felt like I was entering another world. The yard was huge, but also simple. And it was country-quiet here. You could hear the birds and the wind rustling through the trees, but that was it. The first time I'd driven all the way to the house and seen how private it was, I'd thought about how great it would be to raise kids here. I had no idea how long Granddaddy had lived here either, but I guessed he hadn't bought the house until after my dad had grown up.

In front of the house, the driveway rounded into a large circle. In the center of the circle was a raised island where a cluster of maple trees stood. As we got closer to the house, I saw something I hadn't seen on my previous visits—a hammock strung between two trees in the center of the small island. As my car slowly swung around the circle, the gently swaying hammock looked as if it was drifting in the air. It was a surreal illusion, and I had to remind myself that it was my car moving, and not the hammock.

I stopped the car in front of the house and peered through the windshield at it. Granddaddy had claimed that he lived in a simple man's house, but it was pretty nice compared to the apartments Jenn and I lived in. It was two stories, and there were skylights intermittently dotting the roof. The house was a color that allowed it to blend into its natural surroundings. The stone walkway leading to the porch had a slight curve to it. Every detail fit perfectly with the next. It was like the house and the grounds, and even the driveway, were at peace and in harmony with each other.

I turned to look at Jenn and she raised her eyebrows. "It's really nice, but I wouldn't want to mow that yard," she said before her expression turned serious. "Ready?"

"As I'll ever be."

We walked towards the house, our footsteps casting impressions into the noisy crushed stones of the driveway. When we stepped onto the walkway it grew quiet again and I thought about that magical place I'd always imagined Granddaddy going to. I'd always thought it was somewhere else, but today, I wondered if maybe it was right here.

I didn't know what I expected to happen. The house had

always been empty before, so I had no reason to think today would be any different. Suddenly, the front door opened. I stopped walking and looked up, bursting with the hope that it was Granddaddy who'd opened the door. A light from inside the house was shining right into my eyes so I couldn't tell who was standing there at first glance.

"Well? Are you going to take all day out there or are you two going to come in? We're burning precious daylight here!"

It sounded like a command, and I could imagine Granddaddy saying it, but it wasn't him. It was Grandma. I didn't remember much about her, but I'd seen a few pictures and she still looked the same except for maybe more grey hair. She was holding something in her left hand and motioned to us with her right.

"Come on you two, step it out!"

She said it with such authority that I wondered if she might have been ex-military too. Jenn and I obediently followed her order and entered Granddaddy's house. It was very strange walking in. I'd always figured it would be under different circumstances and I wasn't sure what to do. Was I supposed to hug her? Or tell her how sorry I was? Or should I come right out and ask her if Granddaddy was really dead?

Grandma didn't seem surprised to see us though. She didn't waste any time with formalities either. She turned, motioned us to follow, and led us from the entryway into a home with a large open living space. I quickly glanced around looking for Granddaddy, but didn't see him, and followed her to the big kitchen island with its dark multi-color countertop surrounded by several tall wicker chairs. I continued to look around, but now it was mostly because I had no idea of what to do or say.

I looked up at the ceiling and recognized that this was a post-and-beam house. The ceiling was actually the upstairs floor with the beams supporting it exposed. I knew this because I'd been reading about architecture lately. The beams were old and rustic, and gleamed where the light hit them. When I looked to Jenn, she was looking around and I could tell from her expression that she really liked what she was seeing. Everything here was warm and inviting, and there were things in this house that we had talked about having in our own house—like the kitchen island we were now standing around.

"Well," Grandma started. "Have a seat," she finished, motioning us to the chairs.

I looked at her with a tight smile, surprised at how much her words reminded me of the way Granddaddy spoke. Her expression changed then, and she intercepted me, hugging me tightly before I could sit.

"I'm sorry." Grandma said finally letting me go. "I didn't mean to startle you. It's just that it's been so many years since I've seen you and I've missed you." She shook her head, a wistful smile changing her expression. "I just can't believe how much you look like your Granddaddy did when he was a young man." Then she lowered her head and shrugged. "For a moment, I felt like I was back in high school looking at my high-school sweetheart."

"Really?" Jenn ventured.

"Really," Grandma affirmed with a matter-of-fact nod of her head.

"I guess that means he was a handsome guy," I offered, trying to lighten the mood. We all chuckled, but we all sounded nervous too.

Grandma sighed. "I'm very glad you two finally made it here. Your Granddaddy was convinced that you'd stop by today, and he wanted me to give you this," she said placing the object she'd been holding in her hand in front of me. "Happy Birthday. It's your Granddaddy's journal."

My eyes widened and my heart raced as I picked up the worn leather-bound book. It was heavy, and the leather was soft to the touch. When I drew back the cover, the front page had

Granddaddy's name on it, written in a precise script that was easy to read. As I gently thumbed through the pages, his handwriting made me cringe thinking about my own journal, wishing I'd taken as much care when I'd written things down. It had never occurred to me that I might want to hand my journal down to my son, or maybe even a grandson someday.

Grandma continued, "Your Granddaddy told me that you'd know what to do with it. He also told me to remind you that readers are leaders. And today, on your birthday, he wanted you to learn that writers are fighters." She nodded her head again as if she was agreeing with Granddaddy's message and leaned towards us conspiratorially, "and that's a good thing!"

I wasn't exactly sure what that meant, but I was going to have to think about it later because Grandma sat up a little straighter and continued, lightly tapping her fingers on the journal's cover.

"In this journal, you'll hear the voice of another birthday boy who was known as a fighter his whole life. Your Granddaddy armed himself with knowledge and used his own pen to keep track of how the things he learned influenced his life. This journal helped him find his way to the man he became. And it wasn't just about fighting in a war, just like it won't always be about wrestling or football for you.

"Books can expose you to wisdom and hope, and help you see the world of possibilities stretching out ahead of you. But writing your own thoughts down in your own journal can help you plan the trip. Writing will help you identify your own strengths and weaknesses. It will also be a record of your progress and success as you make the journey."

I nodded my head, already in possession of this truth. I wanted to start reading Granddaddy's journal right then and there, but Grandma cleared her throat. I looked at her and saw a resigned expression on her face.

"Okay," Grandma declared. "That's it for now. I'm so sorry to have to say goodbye so quickly, but there's so much that I have to get done right now, and I know you two will understand that. It was nice to finally get a chance to meet you Jenn. Granddaddy said he had a feeling about you. And now that I've met you, I can see exactly what he meant." Then she turned to me. "And you... the last thing Granddaddy said to me about you was that he truly believed you'd be better than fine. Okay then," she said resolutely. "I've got things to do." And with that, Grandma stood, turned, and headed up the stairs to the second floor without a backward glance.

We sat there staring after her wondering if she was going to come back.

"Should we leave?" Jenn asked.

I shrugged, not sure what we should do either. I was holding the journal in both hands now, hopeful because of the amazing gift I'd just received, but very disappointed too. I hadn't had time to ask Grandma any questions about Granddaddy.

"Dakota," Jenn said quietly. "We can't just sit here forever."

I shrugged again, stood, and headed for the front door. Jenn followed, turning a full circle with her departing steps, to take in the cozy home once more before we left.

8.

The Journal

"I am enamored of my journal."

— Sir Walter Scott

When we got into the car, I sat with Granddaddy's journal in my hands. It was heavy, and it felt like an important book. It looked old and used, but was still in great shape, something I'd expect from Granddaddy. It reminded me of the kind of book someone would put on their desk so it was always within easy reach. Or a book that would have been carefully placed on a shelf in the personal library of some famous historical figure.

I bet Granddaddy would have thought of it as a "simple man's journal." I looked up and through the windshield to the yard and then to the house. With each visit over the past year, an impression of Granddaddy had been taking shape in my mind. His home, his yard, and even this book might be old, but they had all been well-taken care of. All of these things looked and felt comfortable too. There was no evidence anywhere of someone trying to keep up with the Jones's. And even though it had been empty all the other times I'd driven here, it had always reminded of a place you could call home.

The cover of the journal was comfortable like that too. It wasn't ornate or flashy. It was too big for my back pocket, but not so big that it would be uncomfortable to carry around. I wanted to open it and start reading it so I could hear Granddaddy's voice in my head as if he was once again speaking to me—with me—on my birthday. The thought of it made my eyes start to burn, but there was no way I was going to let my emotions take over. This wasn't the right time or place for that, so I put the journal on the back seat, started the car, and slowly followed the driveway past the drifting hammock and the cedar trees until I was at the road. For some reason, I put my left blinker on and turned in the opposite direction of the way we came.

"Is this another way back?" Jenn asked.

I shrugged. "I don't know where this road goes. But we've got plenty of gas," I said with a smile that quickly faded away. "The truth is... I'm just not ready to go back yet. I came here hoping to get some answers, but it didn't feel right to ask Grandma any questions about Granddaddy... And, when you think about it, she never said anything about him being... gone."

"Maybe not, but you could tell she was sad," Jenn pointed out.

I nodded my head. "You're right. She did seem sad, but we don't know why. I want to think about this. I want to look at the journal too. After all, she did say that he had asked her to give it to me today. He'd even known we were both going to show up!"

"Yeah. That was kind of eerie. How did he know we were going to do that?"

"I don't know, but if it's a clue, I want to figure it out."

Jenn nodded her head. "Agreed... Do you have any idea where this road goes?"

"Nope."

We rode in silence while a strange war was taking place inside my head. In one sense, I was struck by how beautiful the scenery along this road was. Right now, the road was straight with beautiful open fields on both sides, but I could see that the road ahead was bordered on both sides by trees. On a normal day, I would have been following Granddaddy's advice and taking in all the beauty we were surrounded by. But today wasn't a normal day. Today was the day I found out that one of the most important people in the world to me might actually be dead. It just didn't seem right to try and blend those two things together.

The hard part was that the only person I could even imagine having a solution for my dilemma was Granddaddy. And whether he was dead or somewhere else, he wasn't here to help me figure this out. I didn't know what was in the journal, but my desire to read it was steadily growing. Would I know how he grew from a boy into a man when I was done reading it? I'd read about "rites of passage." For kids, it was when they moved from being considered a boy or girl to being considered a man or woman. I already felt like a man, but even I knew there was more to being a man than just shaving or being old enough to take care of myself.

Now I thought of my day with Granddaddy as a rite of passage. He'd taken me into his world of knowledge and ideas and treated me like I had every right to be there with him and to know this stuff. In fact, he made it clear that I needed to understand the things he was sharing with me. So far, he'd been right about everything, and I would have given just about anything to hear his thoughts on how I should deal with what I was thinking and feeling right now. What would he say?

And then, I felt something I hadn't expected to feel. I was angry. I was angry that he left me with only half the story. I'd gotten started, and I was on a good track, but now I was suddenly feeling the weight of having to do the rest on my own and it really ticked me off—especially if he wasn't actually dead. It reminded me of Pops saying how selfish Granddaddy had always been and how everything had always been about him.

Could it be true? If Granddaddy wasn't dead, was he really just off somewhere chasing his own success like Pops said? Was that what was actually happening right now?

"I don't buy it," I said out loud without thinking.

"What?" Jenn asked.

I looked at her. "I just don't believe that Granddaddy would be selfish enough to pretend to be dead. That's what Pops would say. If I said that I thought Granddaddy might not actually be... gone, he'd say that if he was faking it, it was because he was getting something out—."

"Dakota!"

"What?"

Jenn pointed at the windshield. I turned and saw the stop sign just ahead and put on the brakes hard. Luckily I hadn't been going that fast so I was able to stop the car. But it was definitely a quick reminder to keep my head in the game.

"Thanks," I said.

"No problem," she said with a chuckle.

We sat at the intersection looking around. We were at a four-way stop in the middle of nowhere, with nowhere specific to be.

"Which way will take us back?" Jenn asked.

I pointed my chin to the left. "I think it's that way." Then I put my right blinker on and turned right.

Jenn nodded and reached forward, turning the radio on. An old Nirvana song was playing, and she sang along quietly, in perfect pitch. I didn't know their songs well enough to sing along, but knew that the lead singer of the band had committed suicide. As bad as my life had been when I was younger, I'd never thought of suicide as an option. For a long time it was probably because I was too young to understand what it was, but even if I had understood, I don't think I would have ever done it. I just wanted what we all wanted—for Pops to stop beating on us. And for better or worse, I was going to stick with my mom and brother, which meant that even though I thought about it plenty, I didn't run away either.

It was the gym and working out that helped me turn the corner to something better. There was no denying that when I started pumping iron it was so I could get strong enough to physically stop Pops. I would have gotten there eventually too except that my brother stopped Pops first, and Pops hasn't touched any of us since that night. I guess I could have stopped working out after that. There were definitely days when I felt like it would be easier to quit than to keep going, but I didn't stop.

The truth was that as soon as I started lifting weights, I started feeling better. Working out, and then sports, gave me something to do—something good to focus on that I had control over. I'd like to think that doing something like this would work for other people too. All they'd have to do is find one good thing to start thinking about, or come up with one good thing they could do. It wouldn't have to be sports. It could be anything really, as long as it gave them something better to think about and do.

Granddaddy would probably say that's the starting piece of the gratitude puzzle. But it's not as if someone has to all-of-a-sudden start feeling grateful for everyone or everything. It's more like finding one small thing to be grateful for today, another thing to be grateful for tomorrow, and so on. Today was definitely a challenging day to think about gratitude, but that didn't change the fact that I had a life full of things to be grateful for.

This time I saw the stop sign ahead of us. I turned to smile at Jenn as I slowed to a stop. As always, she smiled back. We were at another four-way stop and I was trying to decide which way to go when Jenn pointed to the right.

"What's that?" she asked.

I had to lean forward to see what she was pointing at. Just beyond a row of trees there was an older stone building with big windows. I didn't know what the building was, but turned right anyway, turned left into the driveway, and then pulled into a parking spot facing the front of the building. Staring up at the entrance, I felt my mouth drop open.

"Does that say what I think it says?" Jenn asked.

"Yup." That was all I could say as we both stared up at the

Kilmartin Memorial Library.

"Isn't Kilmartin Granddaddy's last name?"

"Yup."

9.

The Free Public Library

"A library is the delivery room for the birth of ideas, a place where history comes to life."

— Norman Cousins

From inside the car, Jenn and I just stared at the impressive stone building in front of us. It was big and very majestic. The entrance was an arch of stones, each one perfectly fitted against another. There was a turret on one corner of the building with warm welcoming light filtering out through tall narrow arched windows.

"Are you going to turn the car off?" Jenn asked.

"Huh?" I responded before absently turning the engine off.

"It looks like a castle," she said. "Not a big one, but it does look like a castle. Do you want to go in?"

"As if anyone could keep me out," I said, giving into the excitement of our discovery.

I picked up Granddaddy's journal, got out of the car, and looked around. There was another stone building across the street, and when I looked down the street I saw a few more. None of those other buildings had the same flare as the library, and I stood marveling at the amount of work it must have taken to build it, wondering where all the stones had come from. Had they all been dug up from somewhere around here? Or had they come from someplace else? It was an old building too, and without any effort I could imagine knights and quests, and was getting medieval goose bumps just thinking about it. It was like stepping out of a time machine into the past and being greeted by things that haven't changed for centuries.

I could understand why Granddaddy would chose to live near a town like this too. I could hear the birds singing. A lady walking out of the library as we were walking up the steps smiled and said hello to us. This felt like a place where a man would have the time and space to hear his own thoughts. Right now, it felt like the perfect place to sit and read Granddaddy's journal so I could learn more about his mysterious life.

I opened the door for Jenn and we stepped into the entryway of the library. It was beautiful. The floor was marble and every opening and window was trimmed with rich dark wood. The check-out desk was straight ahead of us. It looked old too, fitting right in with its surroundings, but I could also see up-to-date technology. A woman with red hair was sitting behind the desk. She looked up as we entered and smiled. Then she tilted her head to one side with a puzzled expression that suddenly turned to a look of recognition.

"I bet you're Dakota," she said with a brilliant smile.

I nodded.

"I thought you might be. And that means you must be Jenn," she said rising from the desk and walking around it to join us. "What do you think?" she asked, raising her hands to the interior of the library.

"It's beautiful," I said. "I've never been here before. We didn't even know it was here... wait... how did you know—"

"Know who you are if you've never been here before? That's easy. Come see," she said turning and taking a few steps towards a wall where she pointed to a small framed picture with a plaque underneath.

I looked at it. It was the same picture of Granddaddy that had accompanied his obituary. Once again, it was like looking into a weird mirror and seeing myself dressed in a uniform that was obviously from another generation. The plaque was very simple. All it said was, "In profound gratitude for your generosity, we hereby name this building the Kilmartin Memorial Library."

"Your grandfather rarely talked about his life, but last week he saw me reading an article about the football play-off game and pointed to your picture. He was busting with pride too. And now that you've seen the picture, you can see how easy it was for me to recognize you. As for you Jenn, Neil mentioned you when he was talking about Dakota. He said the two of you made a good team, and it was obvious how proud he was of both of you."

I saw Jenn blush. "Me?" she asked very quietly.

"Absolutely. He said you were just as full of potential as Dakota was, and that you were a good influence on him."

I took Jenn's hand and gave it a squeeze. "He's right about that."

"He also said that you might stop by today, and that when you did I should introduce myself and show you around. Oh," she said realizing and extending her hand, "I'm Mary Reynolds."

"Reynolds?" I asked.

"Yes," she answered.

"Have you ever heard of a man named Colonel Reynolds?" I asked hoping for another coincidence—that might not be a coincidence at all.

"Of course," she answered. "He was my Grandfather," she said proudly, "and your Grandfather's company commander during WWII."

I blinked fiercely, trying not to get too choked up with the gratitude I was suddenly feeling for her Grandfather. I didn't know if he was the reason Granddaddy made it through the war, but he had helped shape Granddaddy's life, and in the end, my life too. Then it hit me that working here, Mary Reynolds probably knew more about Granddaddy than I did. "So, you saw a lot of Granddaddy?" I asked, trying to hide how quickly my thoughts had switched from gratitude to jealousy.

Her expression changed. "Not really. That conversation about you two was probably the longest one I ever had with him. Of course, there were plenty of memos and emails because he was on the board of directors for the library, but when he came in he usually just waived and headed straight for his favorite chair to read, or to work on his laptop. So it was more like I got to say hello and goodbye as he came and went. He was always very nice though. And... I was really sorry to hear that... well... you know."

I nodded. I did know. "But he told you we were going to be here today?" I asked, suddenly feeling bad about being jealous even for just a few seconds.

"He told me last Thursday that you might stop by either today or tomorrow, and here you are. Can I give you the grand tour?"

Jenn and I both nodded our heads, and we followed Mary around as she pointed out different things. I was only half listening though, thinking about the fact that Granddaddy had pinpointed the days we might stop in. In my head, that was solid evidence that he'd known my investigation into his death would lead us here.

She showed us around the first floor, and then took us up the stairs to tour the second floor, ending in the corner turret room. The room was open, but it was set up as a cozy spot to read. The view through the window was peaceful, and when I looked at the two overstuffed chairs facing it, I suddenly felt very tired and sat down in one of them.

Mary stared at me with a suspicious expression on her face. "Are you sure you've never been here?"

"Never," I said.

"Well how 'bout that. That chair was your grandfather's favorite place to sit."

I stood quickly and turned to look at the chair. I don't know what I expected to see. It wasn't like I'd sat on somebody or something—the chair was as empty as it had been before I sat in it. Maybe it was because Granddaddy had predicted that I'd be here. It made me think that I should be looking for a clue, and if this was his favorite place to sit, then maybe he'd left me a clue here.

"When he came to the library, this is where he sat. Then he was like a man on a mission. He read all sorts of books but seemed to lean towards biographies of successful people. It was his theory that success is something we can plan for. In fact, there's one more thing I want to show you."

Mary led us to two tall book racks by the stairs. Between them was another plaque. This one said, "Don't leave your success to chance. Study people from the past and the present, and use the lessons, insights, knowledge, and wisdom you find as a guide for creating your future."

I started reading the book titles and recognized three books I'd read this past year: To Kill a Mockingbird, The Grapes of Wrath, and The Great Gatsby. There were book titles that I had on my reading list too, but there were so many others that I'd never even heard of. And right at that moment, I wished things were different so I could pull a few of them off the shelf and sit down and start reading them right now.

"What's really interesting about these books," she continued, "is that they can each be found in their proper location in the library too. But it was one of your grandfather's desires to have a special section where someone could go to find a book that would inspire them, or maybe help them grow. If you look at the spines, you'll see that each book has blue dot on it. That's how we know if a book belongs here, or in its proper location in the stacks. Whenever he found a book he wanted to add to this collection, he would bring in two copies. One for the stacks, and one for the success library. I think that's the reason he liked to sit here. He could look out the window and enjoy the view, and still see these books."

That sounded like Granddaddy to me. He could sit here and watch the people who stood in front of the success books. Maybe he sent them some good vibes or something, but even if he never talked to any of them, it was still a way for him to lend a helping hand to someone he'd never actually met. And I could absolutely see him sitting in that chair reading, lost in a thoughtful meditation about what he could learn, so he could then turn around and help someone else. Just standing there between Granddaddy's success library and his favorite chair made me feel closer to him.

Mary pointed to the table where I had rested Granddaddy's journal. "I see you brought something to read, so I'll leave you to it," she said, turning to leave and then abruptly turning back. "I'm sorry, I almost forgot. You're grandfather asked me to give this to you when you came in." She reached into one of the pockets in her sweater and pulled out a sealed envelope.

"Thanks," I said taking it from her.

After she'd gone, Jenn and I sat on the edge of the overstuffed chairs, staring at the envelope. My name was on the front, but that was it. I took a deep breath, opened it, and pulled out a single sheet of paper, holding it out so we could both read what it said.

I spent many hours sitting in my favorite chair in this library thinking about what I'd say to you in this note. First, and most of all, I'm proud of you and the man you are becoming. I'm proud of you too Jenn – and have no doubt that you're sitting right next to Dakota reading this. One of my few regrets is that I didn't have the privilege of officially meeting you.

Hopefully, you are now in possession of my first journal too. I wanted you to have it Dakota. You and Jenn will be the only people who've ever read it. But before you get carried away thinking about what's inside it, there aren't any state secrets, or any kind of information like that. It's just the first journal I started writing towards the end of the war.

Every day was a challenge for us in the war. We were truly blessed to have a man like Colonel Reynolds to guide and inspire us, but most of it would have been lost to me if I hadn't written it down. A strange thing happens to people when the worst is behind them. There's a part of them that wants to forget all of it so they can move on. But if history has taught us anything, it's taught us that when we choose to forget and/or ignore the past, it's destined to repeat itself.

I wanted to forget the gory details, but there was much more to what I experienced than that. I struggled with myself—with trying to be a better, stronger, more courageous man than I felt like at the time. And if there's one thing I'm grateful for, it's that so far, you have not had to find your way in the middle of an armed conflict. I have no doubt that you could though. Many a great leader was born under those circumstances, but surviving those kinds of difficulties alone does not make a man a better man. That is the result of choice.

In my journal you're going to recognize when I struggled with the whole idea of choice. It's not always easy to understand the role choice plays until you get to that point where you can truly stop and acknowledge that who you are—or aren't—is always the result of the choices you've made. I know you understand this Dakota, and I know that you are committed to making choices that will have you growing and going in a meaningful and purposeful direction. Congratulations in advance."

I folded the letter, put it back in its envelope, and slipped it inside the front cover of Granddaddy's journal. I wanted to open the journal too, but just couldn't. It was too real now. When I'd first held the journal in my hands at Granddaddy's house, I'd felt a rush of expectation and excitement thinking it was a book full of his advice and knowledge. Now I understood that reading it wasn't going to be like that day in the park with Granddaddy. It was going to be his thoughts, in real time, when he was just a couple of years older than I was now.

Jenn and I sat quietly looking out the window watching late November clouds race across the sun and sky. I hadn't found any answers to my questions today. Was Granddaddy alive? I had no idea. This note made me think he might be, but Grandma hadn't looked happy, and Mary Reynolds had said she was sorry about Granddaddy.

My brain hurt trying to juggle all the pieces of the puzzle I was trying to solve. I had no idea what to think or feel, and just wanted some time away from all of it.

"Ready?" I asked, looking into Jenn's reassuring brown eyes.

She shrugged and smiled her gentle smile. "Ready when you are."

10.

The Funeral

Emperor Meiji: "Tell me how he died."
Algren: "I will tell you how he lived."
— Scene from Last Samurai Movie

Three days later, Jenn and I were sitting in my car outside the funeral home. The past few days had been strange. When I got home on Saturday, my mom let me know the funeral was going to be on Tuesday. Those had been hard words to hear, one more piece of evidence stacking up in the wrong direction. I couldn't think of anywhere else to look for clues either. I tried to read Granddaddy's journal but just wasn't ready to go there yet.

Monday morning my mom told me I didn't have to go to school if I didn't feel up to it, but I didn't want to stay home. Pops was there. He'd gotten drunk the night before, and my mom had called his boss that morning to let him know there'd been a death in the family, and that Pops would be out for the next few days.

I went to school instead, grateful to know that Jenn would be there too. As near as I could tell, no one else knew my grandfather had died. I went to all my classes but none of the teachers said anything out of the ordinary to me. None of my friends said anything either, but they don't read the newspaper so I didn't expect them to know. It was as if Jenn and I were the only ones who knew or cared about Granddaddy, and it was just plain strange how normally the days leading up to the funeral passed by. There were even a couple of moments when I found myself

61

almost smiling at something funny, and then I'd stop because something didn't feel right. Then I'd remember that Granddaddy was gone.

I still wasn't sure how I was supposed to feel. Was there a right way to feel? It didn't seem to matter because the world kept right on hustling around me. Part of me was still trying to hold on to the idea that he might be alive, but there weren't any reasons why I should. Maybe it was better to just let him go. Was I really doing myself any favors believing he might be alive? And if he really was gone, I knew the last thing he'd want for me was to waste my time wishing for something I didn't have any control over. If he was gone, he was gone, and that was that.

When Jenn and I got to the funeral home, we sat in the car and watched the parking lot fill up. I noticed that a bunch of the cars had government plates. There were two cars that had Homeland Security seals on their doors too. I'd never even thought to ask Granddaddy if he was still in the military. He'd never said anything about it one way or the other either.

"I guess it's time to go in," I said, checking the time on my phone for about the 50th time. Neither of us had ever been to "viewing hours" before so we didn't know what to expect. When we walked through the front door, there were three rooms to choose from, but I could tell which room was for Granddaddy right away because I could see Grandma talking to a man in a uniform. There were several other men in uniform too. When we walked into the room, people were quick to look in our direction, and then just as quick to look away. I looked around but didn't recognize anybody. I knew Pops wouldn't be here. Without having work as an excuse to stay sober, he'd been drinking steadily for the past few days and was in no shape to go anywhere. I think my mom would have come if Pops had, but not on her own. My brother wasn't here either. In fact, I hadn't seen him since Saturday.

When Grandma saw Jenn and me she smiled a sad smile and held her hands out to us. We walked to her, but I didn't know what I was supposed to do or say this time either. Was I supposed to hug her? Was I supposed to say what they always say on TV, "I'm sorry for your loss."

"Dakota, Jenn, thank you so much for coming today. I know your Granddaddy would very much appreciate the fact that you came," she said giving us each a hug in turn. Then she turned to the man she'd been speaking to. "Colonel Smith, this is my grandson Dakota and his friend Jenn."

Colonel Smith extended his hand to Jenn first, and then to me. "It's nice to meet both of you," he said, his handshake sure and strong.

"Thank you Sir," I said, hoping it was the right thing to say.

"Please excuse me," the Colonel said turning to Grandma.

"Of course... and thank you for all your help," Grandma said in response. She watched the Colonel walk away and turned back to us. "I don't suppose you know any of the people here," she said looking around. "To be honest, I don't know many of them either—not personally at any rate. But it's been nice hearing about some of the things you're Granddaddy did for the people here. It's nice knowing that that's how people will remember him too.... He was a good man," she said, her voice shaking, her eyes tearing.

I nodded in agreement, my throat too tight to say anything.

"Well," Grandma said, clearing her throat and moving to one side. "I'll leave you two to pay your respects."

I looked past Grandma and saw an easel holding a huge picture of Granddaddy dressed in uniform. It wasn't the picture I'd seen in the newspaper though. This picture was of an older Granddaddy. I expected to see a casket too, but instead saw a copper-colored urn sitting on top of a low pedestal table with a folded American flag resting next to it.

Grandma must have seen the look on my face. "You're Granddaddy was cremated," she said matter-of-factly. "It was what he wanted."

I just nodded, and then Jenn and I took the few steps forward.

"Is that what he looked like?" Jenn asked quietly.

I nodded.

"I wondered what he looked like. I wondered if when I got to meet him I'd remember having seen him at one of your matches or games. Or maybe I'd have remembered him from somewhere else. But I don't think I've ever seen him before. He looks nice though."

We stood there for a while, neither of us really sure how long we were supposed to stand there. There was a tall narrow glass cabinet to the left of the portrait, and we moved over to look at it. In it were displayed different things from Granddaddy's life. There were old military photos of him standing with other people, and I wondered if one of the people was Colonel Reynolds. One shelf was used to display his medals and ribbons. It was an impressive display. I didn't know what they stood for except for the three I remembered learning about in history class: a Purple Heart, a Bronze Star, and a Silver Star.

The last two shelves had books on them. They'd obviously been read many times over. One of them was laid open to reveal two pages full of underlined sentences and notes in the margins. I stepped closer and read the title. It was, "How to Win Friends and Influence People" by Dale Carnegie. Were these Granddaddy's favorite books? I looked at the other books on the shelves too, trying to commit their titles to memory. The Art of War by Sun Tzu, The Last Tycoon by F. Scott Fitzgerald, Siddhartha by Hermann Hesse, Pride and Prejudice by Jane Austen, and Crime and Punishment by Fyodor Dostoyevsky.

We stood there for a few minutes and then turned back towards the room full of people. Grandma was talking to another man in uniform. He had a lot of medals too, and I wondered how he knew Granddaddy. Grandma had said that most of the people there were there because Granddaddy had helped them in some way. I knew he'd been in the military, but wondered what he'd done to help Homeland Security.

Jenn pointed to two empty chairs towards the back of the room and we made our way to them, relieved to sit. "How are you doing?" she asked quietly.

I shrugged. "Okay I guess... but there sure are a lot of guys in uniform here."

"Yeah.... I noticed that too. Maybe he was in the reserve or something."

"I don't know," I said, leaning in and lowering my voice even more. "Did you see that?" I asked, discretely pointing at the three soldiers standing in front of Granddaddy's ashes. "Did those soldiers just salute Granddaddy's ashes?"

"They did. What do you think that means?"

"I don't know."

I looked around for Grandma and saw her standing off to one side. I took hold of Jenn's hand, stood, and walked to Grandma.

"Grandma," I started, my voice low, "Was Granddaddy still in the military?"

A surprised look took over her face. "Of course. He was a Colonel. He could have retired a long time ago, but he loved this country so much he would have done anything for it. It was another one of those things that made your Granddaddy so special."

"I didn't know," I said. "I mean.... I knew he'd been in the military, I just thought he was retired."

"I'm not surprised. But I'm sure there are other people here who didn't realize he was a Colonel either. He didn't talk about it unless there was a reason to. And," she said, leaning towards them, "truth be told, he didn't spend a lot time in uniform."

I nodded gravely, not sure if that meant something or not. "Okay you two…. I really appreciate you coming here today, but it's time for you to leave. You've spent enough time here, and I know Granddaddy would prefer that you were out there living rather than hanging around here. So scoot!"

I smiled at my wonderful Grandma, filled with hope that I might see her again. Then I gave her a big hug, absolutely sure that it was the right thing to do. "Thanks Grandma."

Part 2

11.

The Odyssey

"Strangers... who are you? And where from?
What brings you here...?"
— The Odyssey Book 9 lines 274-275

Tweeeep! (whistle blowing)

When I got up from the mat, I slowly rolled my head from side to side. My opponent had wrenched it pretty good during the match and it was going to be sore tomorrow, but that was tomorrow. Right now, my heart was pounding and I was breathing hard from both exhaustion and exhilaration.

When my opponent stood, I was reminded that he was a couple of inches taller than me. That would account for a couple of the moves he was able to execute—height equals leverage if you know how to take advantage of it. There'd even been a moment when I'd almost given into thinking that his extra height might stack the odds in his favor, but then I brought my thoughts right back to focusing solely on what I knew I had control over. I couldn't control what he was going to try to do to me. I could only control what I did, and I'd been working hard to make sure I was both mentally and physically prepared to take quick and efficient action when the opportunity presented itself. I'd done a lot of purposeful work leading up to this day, and I was ready to do battle to the end because of it.

As we stepped back into the center of the wrestling mat, I surveyed my opponent. He looked whipped. I was feeling the effects of the match too, but stood straight and tall and extended my hand to him. We shook, and then the whistle-blowing referee dressed in the traditional zebra-colored shirt grabbed my right arm and extended it into the air. I could feel the burn of the lactic acid running through the veins of my arm, but I didn't care. Instead, I listened to the cheers and clapping of the crowd, taking in every second of it. This wasn't the only reason I wrestled, but hearing the roars and cheers of the spectators was definitely one of my favorite perks.

I kept my expression respectful while I was standing there, but as soon as I turned away I felt a huge smile take over my face. He'd been a tough opponent, but I'd been tougher, and now I was one step closer to achieving my goal. I didn't know who my next opponent was yet, but he would be a strong opponent too—everyone here was strong.

This tournament was a preseason invitation-only event. To get an invitation, you had to be a state champ or a place-winner. That meant that everyone here had earned their invitation by being one of the best high school wrestlers in their state. Right now, we were all competing to earn a spot as one of the eight All-American wrestlers in our weight class. Then, when the All-American rounds started, we'd be competing against each other for the top spot on the awards podium, and the title of National Champion for our weight class.

I'd earned my invitation by winning last year's state wrestling championship. I was feeling confident, but I needed to stay focused on each match if I wanted to win. I needed two more wins to make it to the All-American rounds. If I could do that, I'd definitely have college wrestling scouts lining up to get my contact information, and that would set another one of my goals in motion—a college wrestling scholarship. Following up my success at this tournament with more wins during both the regular high school wrestling season, and then the post-season tournaments, would definitely result in a wrestling scholarship!

My private goal for this tournament was to be standing at the top of the podium at the end of the day. It wasn't really a secret; both Jenn and Coach knew that was what I was shooting for. In my head though, it was hard to separate wanting to win from what I had to do to win. I could see myself standing up there. I'd been closing my eyes and imagining standing up there more times than I could count. I could feel the exhilaration of standing there. It was a great feeling, but I remembered what Granddaddy had said about what we can control and what we can't. He had said that sometimes, even when we do our best, we fail. I understood what he was saying too, but I just had this feeling that I couldn't fail today. This was my day. I had worked and planned and executed every little bit of the success I'd experienced so far. This was just another step along the way.

I looked up to where I knew Jenn was sitting. She was clapping and hooting just as loud as everybody else. My mom was there too. She wasn't quite as animated as Jenn was, but she was smiling from ear-to-ear and clapping, and it made me feel good that she was there. She'd come to all of my football games this season too.

The first couple of times she'd been there she'd come up to me after the game and gotten all teary-eyed telling me how proud she was of me. Fortunately she figured out I wasn't going to stick around for that. It wasn't that I didn't appreciate the words. It was the exact opposite. Her words meant the world to me. But if I stood around listening to them, I'd get teary-eyed too and there was no way was I going to let the guys see that! Instead, when I got home, I always gave her a big hug and thanked her for coming to the game.

I think I understood why she started coming. This past summer, on July 5th, my brother died in a motorcycle accident. We'd both lost someone we cared about and it was hard for us to deal with. In a very real way, my brother saved my life—maybe my mom's too. He'd gotten physically big enough to stop Pops from beating on us before I did. The fight between them had been brutal, but it was my brother who was standing at the end of it. Pops never came after us after that night. My brother was never the same after it though.

Now it was like my mom and I had to stick together. Pops never came to a game with her, but he hadn't tried to stop her either. After my brother died, he just kind of climbed into a hole and hasn't showed any signs of climbing out. For a while, I was worried he might start up again, but both my mom and I pretty much steered clear of him, and so far, so good.

My coach had a big smile on his face, and gave me a congratulatory high five.

"Who's next?" I asked.

He shook his head. "Don't know yet. I saw your neck get tweaked. How is it?"

I rolled it around so he could see. "Fine." I was feeling too good to feel any pain anyway.

"Okay. Be back here in 45 minutes."

That was one of the things I really appreciated about my coach. He knew that after winning the match I'd want to be by myself for a while. It was one of my rituals. I liked taking time to sit and feel good about what had happened, and then to refocus and prepare for what would be required of me next.

I nodded to him, pulled on my sweats, grabbed my backpack, and headed over to where Jenn and my mom were standing.

"That was really impressive!" Mom said with a smile.

"Thanks," I said, smiling at the reminder that today was my 18th birthday.

"One down," Jenn said looking into my eyes.

"One down," I repeated looking back at her.

"When's your next match," Mom asked.

Jenn answered for me. "In about an hour... if everything stays on schedule."

"Okay... well, I know you have stuff to do, and I saw a coffee shop around the corner, so I'm going to go there and catch up on my reading," she said, reaching into her purse and pulling out a thick paperback book. "I brought this with me figuring we'd all be here for a while. See you in about an hour then," she added before turning and heading towards the exit.

When she was gone, Jenn smiled at me. "Go ahead. I'll be here when you come out," she said pulling a book of her own out of her bag.

I loved Jenn for that. She never tried to intrude when I was doing my thing. Sometimes it was like we spoke the same language without saying anything at all. I turned and headed for the locker room, my thoughts already starting to focus on the task ahead. As I walked, I heard people saying things like, "Good job," "I knew you could do it," and "He was a tough one! Way to go kid!" It was nice to hear, and I confess to maybe walking a little slower so I could listen to their voices.

Maybe it was stupid, and I knew it wasn't possible, but there was still a part of me that refused to give up the hope of hearing Granddaddy's voice. After all, he'd told me about all the times he'd hidden in plain sight to watch me at a football game or a wrestling match. He'd explained that he needed to keep a low profile. And even though I never saw him, it was comforting to know that he might be watching. I'd listened for his voice all through my junior year football season too, but that was different. That was before his obituary.

After his funeral I looked for him everywhere. All through my junior year wrestling season, Jenn and I kept a lookout for him— or for a clue he might leave for us—but there was nothing. There were a few times when I thought I saw him, but as soon as I got close enough to see that it wasn't him it was like getting kicked in the gut all over again. And it was exhausting. I almost lost the wrestling match that made it possible for me to go to the state championships last year because I thought I saw Granddaddy in the stands and completely lost my focus. I won the match, but just barely, and that was when I realized I had to stop looking and listening for him.

This year it was easier not to always be looking for Granddaddy. Maybe it was because my brother had died. Now there were two voices I was never going to hear again. My brother had been there for me before Granddaddy, and I honestly didn't know if I would have made it this far if it hadn't been for him. It was just so hard to accept that his life had ended like that. He was only 20 years old.

12.

Mentors and Lessons Learned

"A mentor is someone who allows you to see the hope inside yourself."

— Oprah Winfrey

I was so angry after my brother died, and all of that anger got directed straight at Pops. Up until that day, I'd been making slow and steady progress in my relationship with him. It wasn't like I was actually trying to connect with him; relationships are two-way streets, and even if I'd wanted to have a real father-son relationship, it was pretty clear he didn't want to have one with me. He never spoke to me before my brother's death—unless it was to tell me to do something—and he didn't speak to me after it. Not one word. He never even looked at me; not even at the funeral.

But I looked at him, angrier than ever. If Pops had been a better person instead of the bullying abuser he was, then my brother might not be dead right now. I wanted to make sure he knew that I was holding him responsible, and that I wasn't going to be anything like him because I was different. All I needed to do was to make eye contact with him so he'd get the message loud and clear. At the very least, I just wanted to see some kind of reaction. Anything that would show he cared. After all, it wasn't just my brother in the casket. It was his son!

It didn't happen. Instead, I noticed something really weird. It wasn't just me that Pops didn't look at. It was everyone. When people talked to him at the funeral he just looked at the floor. Sometimes he nodded his head, but that was it. When people tried to have a conversation with him he just grunted or shrugged his shoulders. He didn't look at anyone—not even if someone shook his hand.

No one at my brother's funeral hugged him either. He just kept his head down most of the time. It was a strange thing to see and I immediately wondered if I avoided looking at people too. The first thing I thought of was sports. In a wrestling match, I always made it a point to look straight at my opponents. I looked them right in the eye too because I wanted them to know that I wasn't afraid— even if I was. That realization freaked me out because it had me flashing back to a time when I'd probably been around seven years old and I'd looked straight into Pops' eyes just before he hit me. His eyes had been almost black, and I never tried to look again.

Did my eyes do that? Did they go black when I stared at an opponent? After thinking about it for a while, I was pretty sure they didn't. There might have been a time when I was close to that, back when I still believed I was going to have to be the one to stop Pops, but definitely not after my brother stepped in.

After my day with Granddaddy, I realized there was still a part of me that wanted Pops to know he would never touch me again. It wasn't like I was looking for a chance to go after him to prove it. It was more like there was still an unspoken "I dare you" hanging in the air between us, and at my brother's funeral that "I dare you" definitely fueled my anger.

Funerals can be strange though. You think about things you'd never think about anywhere else. I thought about the fact that I wasn't ever going to talk to my brother again, and definitely tried to avoid thinking about the truth that I hadn't really talked to him in at least three months. I guess I'd been too busy. I wasn't sure if the funeral would have been easier if we'd had a great talk the day before the accident, but we hadn't, and that was on me, not Pops. And for about the millionth time, I wondered what Granddaddy would have to say.

Fortunately, I was getting better at coming up with answers on my own. I needed to remember the difference between what I could and couldn't control, and that the only thing I really had any control over was myself. I didn't have any control over my brother's choice to ride his motorcycle, and I would never have control over what Pops did or didn't do. What I did have control over was the choice of whether or not I wanted to keep butting my head against that brick wall.

So, after my brother's funeral, I decided I didn't want to walk around feeling like there was some kind of unspoken challenge hanging in the air between Pops and me, and from that moment forward, I made every effort to drop my end of it. If I ever needed to, I could defend myself, but it suddenly felt like a huge waste of my time and energy to always be worrying or anticipating or expecting that I might have to do it right then and there. It was sort of like what Teddy Roosevelt said about speaking softly and carrying a big stick.

After I made that decision I realized just how stressed I got when Pops was around. It was like a constant tension I'd grown so used to that it had stopped registering. It took a while to stop feeling the effects of it too. First, I had to recognize it when it was happening. I think I noticed it in my gut first—like when he came home and I heard him at the front door. My gut would clench tight. And then I'd hold my breath listening for signs that he was drunk.

It was really tough in the beginning too, but now that I'd decided I wasn't going to give one ounce of my power away to him, I realized something else. I realized I was feeling two things in those moments. One was fear. I'd been terrified of him when I was little—especially after that time I'd made eye contact with him. Was I still afraid of him now? Not really. I knew I could defend myself if I had to. And truthfully, he wouldn't have been much of an opponent. I was in great shape. He was still a big guy, but I'd taken down bigger guys than him before.

As I'd gotten older, I used anger to overcome my fear, because it was easier to be angry than it was to be scared. Anger just felt more powerful than fear. But I'd learned early in sports that anger doesn't help performance, it interferes with it. With sports, the goal is to get into the zone, and both anger and fear will pull you out of the zone faster than anything. I think Granddaddy would probably say that anger and fear can pull you right out of your own life too.

Every time I'd felt one of those two feelings around Pops, it was like I was getting sucked right out of my zone. It got easier after I figured that out. It came down to making a decision about which experience I wanted to have. Did I want to feel all that anxiety when Pops was around? Obviously I didn't. The solution was to feel something different.

For me, that different feeling was to know that I could make the decision not to get caught up in Pops' crap. I didn't actually know what Pops was thinking, or what he was feeling, and there wasn't anything I could do about it anyway. I just knew that I didn't want to waste anymore of my time being afraid of him, or feeling like I had to physically prove to him that what I was thinking and feeling was more important than what he was thinking and feeling. He'd made his choices, and now it was time for me to make mine. I no longer needed to make eye contact so I could stare him down to prove it either. I wasn't going to follow his path. I wasn't going to make the same choices, or the same mistakes. I was going to do better.

So I stopped acting like I needed to make eye contact with him to prove myself. And fortunately for me, I could make eye contact with people that felt good. I've looked into Jenn's eyes a million times and never seen or felt anything that even remotely resembled anger or fear. With Jenn, it was like we were talking without words. I'd been able to look into my mom's eyes too— which is a very weird thing to experience. With her, it was warm and comforting. But that was how it should be with a mom. Our moms make us feel good in different ways.

I've heard the saying, "the eyes are a window to the soul" before. But I'd never thought about what it meant. I'd never realized how many chances there are to look people in the eye either. Of course there were plenty of times when it wasn't a good idea to look someone in the eye—well, at least in my neighborhood.

I guess it came down to when you wanted to make a real connection with someone. Looking someone in the eye was a way to let them know a little bit about yourself, starting with the fact that you respected them enough to look them in the eye. When I looked my opponents in the eye, it was to let them know that I was confident, and that I was focusing all my intention and energy into doing what I had to do to win. But in a way, I was welcoming them to give me their best too.

With Jenn, it was always a way of letting her know how much I loved her, appreciated her, and how much of a difference she made in my life. With my friends and teammates—not that we went around looking into each other's eyes—it was like we were establishing a sense of camaraderie.

Looking into someone's eyes gives us an idea of what it might be like to spend time with that person. If someone isn't willing to make eye contact, it's going to be tougher to get to know them. It might be because they're too shy, but it might also be because they aren't interested in connecting. And it's not like you can force a connection on someone who isn't interested. It just doesn't work that way.

I didn't know if I would have figured all that out if I hadn't been at my brother's funeral. Maybe... but there was no way to know for sure. Granddaddy had said he was sure that my brother wanted me to succeed, and that if he hadn't cared, he wouldn't have stepped in to stop Pops. And Granddaddy was right. My brother could have just runaway and left me and my mom to fend for ourselves. He didn't. He stayed and fought for all of us and I wasn't ever going to forget that. I hated being at his funeral, but I was truly grateful for all the things I started to figure out while I was sitting there.

13.

Passing the Secrets Forward

"Share your knowledge. It's a way to achieve immortality."

— Dalai Lama

In the locker room, I sat down, pulled my journal out of my backpack, and flipped it open to a page where I'd written down two quotes to help me stay focused today. Normally, I'd have only written down one quote, but today was special enough to have two. I'd gotten into the habit of writing down quotes last year after Granddaddy's funeral. I'd started reading a lot more, and every time I read something that reminded me of something Granddaddy would say, I wrote it down. Now, whenever I was facing a challenge, I'd go through my favorite quotes and find ones that fit the challenge I was facing. The first of today's quotes was:

"Gold medals aren't really made of gold. They're made of sweat, determination, and a hard-to-find alloy called guts."

Dan Gable said that. He was a retired American Gold Medal Olympic Wrestler. He was also the head wrestling coach at the University of Iowa where his team won 15 NCAA team titles between 1976 and 1997. I liked this quote because I knew I had the guts to see this day through no matter what the outcome was. I was here to do my best, and I had the guts to leave it all on the mat if that's what it was going to take to win. The next quote was:

81

A Sprint to the Top

"Accept the challenges so that you can feel the exhilaration of victory."

George S. Patton Jr. said this one. He was a general who commanded the U.S. Seventh Army in the Mediterranean and European Theaters of World War II. It was here to remind me of the challenges I'd had to face over the past couple of years. They weren't all there by choice—like the challenge of dealing with two people in my life dying—and there'd been times when I'd been tempted to give up. I don't think anyone would have blamed me if I'd given up either. The people around me were used to giving up, so it was more like I was different because I didn't. And sure, people can still win without doing the work, but how good can that feel? My wins are the result of me facing up to and overcoming my challenges. Today was just another in a series of challenges between me and the winner's podium.

I liked quotes because there weren't many people in my life I could look up to. I had great coaches and teachers who I'd learned a lot from, but quotes accomplished something else. They put me in touch with people who succeeded big time. And that's what I was aiming for… "big time" success. Granddaddy had been a huge help, but he was gone and it was up to me to choose my role models. So I really appreciated it when I found a quote by someone I admired. Most of the time, the quotes I wrote down were spoken by people I wasn't likely to bump into. For me, their words were inspiration. For them, their words were a way to give back.

I wouldn't have thought about it that way if Granddaddy hadn't told me that I was going to start giving back at some point too. Even after he said it I'd thought he meant sometime later in my life when I was settled into my career. Now I know different. Last spring, I was outside of my apartment building and saw a group of kids hanging out. It was like looking at myself and the guys I used to hang out with when I was their age. It made me smile, but it also got me thinking about who they had to look up to. Did they have someone in their life they could talk to or who would listen to their questions? I didn't know the answer and wondered if I could help.

So I started talking to them about sports. At first, I didn't say a whole lot. They didn't want to hear me talking anyway. I heard about their favorite sports and about their sports heroes. After they figured out how much I was into sports too, they started asking me questions. I got to tell them about playing football and being a wrestler, and about the championships I'd won as part of a team and as an individual.

Pretty soon we were talking—really talking—about things that could make a difference. The interesting part of those conversations was that I didn't always have a deep understanding of what we were really talking about until we started talking. Then, somehow, just by trying to do a good job of explaining, I managed to figure out how things worked at a deeper level along the way. Like when I totally understood that talking to them about making the decision to bring their best to a competition was a stepping stone to them realizing that they could make the decision to bring their best into their own life too.

We talked about what it was like being part of a team, and about the reality that sometimes it was hard to stay friends with people. I barely ever talked to any of the people I'd hung around with when I was their age. We'd just gone in different directions. Some of my old friends had gone towards the gangs, and I knew some of these kids would join gangs too. But maybe if they understood a little bit more about how our choices shape our lives, it would help them when it came time for them to make some of those tough choices.

I told them the story about the bucket of crabs, and about how fishermen say that you should never put just one crab in a bucket, because if you do, it could climb up the side of the bucket and escape. The trick is to make sure there are at least two crabs in the bucket. That way, when the bottom crab tries to escape by climbing over the higher crab, their combined weight is too much and they both end up falling back to the bottom of the bucket. If the crabs in the bucket were capable of working together, they might be able to escape their fate. But they can't because they're just crabs, and crabs don't know how to work together.

Then I explained the difference between crabs and people. People have the ability to look at who they're "stuck in a bucket" with. People always have a choice about whether or not to sacrifice a teammate or a friend when they're trying to get ahead too. Unfortunately, there are times when people will hold others back from escaping their shared circumstances, even when those circumstances are really bad.

It was easy to like those neighborhood kids, and I made it a point to stop and talk to them when I could because I wanted them to believe in themselves more than I'd believed in myself when I was their age. I even played a little football with them. I didn't know if talking to them would make a difference, but I could see the looks on their faces when they tried to understand something I said. They were listening.

I tried not to sound too much like an adult when I encouraged them to think about things. But I still challenged them to ask themselves what the right thing to do was, and to stay out of trouble. It felt good that they listened and sometimes even followed my advice. I'd learned so much from Granddaddy and was quick to recognize that this was an opportunity to help shape our small corner of the world into a better place. But I learned from them too. One of the biggest things was that now I knew I hadn't been the only kid experiencing what I'd gone through. I probably already knew that on some level, but hearing these kids talk really put it in perspective.

Taking on the role of being a big brother type "mentor" felt good, but it was a challenge because they were always watching me. For all I knew, I was one of the first people they'd ever actually listened to and I was determined not to disappoint them. That meant walking the walk, because if I didn't, I'd lose their respect in a heartbeat. So I made sure to bring my "A" game when I was around them.

I enjoyed telling them about "self-fulfilling prophecies," and explained how I'd started creating my own self-fulfilling prophecies when I was around their age. I was honest and talked about some of the mistakes I'd made along the way too, to prove to them that making mistakes didn't make someone a failure. Not getting up and trying to do better the next time... that was the only real mistake. And sometimes that meant putting your head down and plowing your way through.

Another thing they heard me say more than once was that if I could do it, then so could they. I made sure they knew that I wasn't special or different or unique. I'd just read a few books, and listened to a couple of coaches and teachers who I could tell really cared. Of course I made sure they understood that I'd started taking charge of my choices too, and that I took responsibility for my actions. They looked at me as if I was speaking a foreign language the first time I said that, but I kept adding it into our conversations when it fit, and they started to get it—especially when it was sports related.

Now it was like we'd all been best friends since the beginning of time. Sometimes one of them would ask me a question when no one else could hear, and we'd talk about it. I was no Granddaddy, but it still felt right to share some of what he shared with me with somebody else.

I heard the locker room door open. Guys had been coming in and out the whole time I'd been in here, but right now the room was empty. Then I heard Jenn's voice.

"Dakota? You in there?"

I looked up at the clock, surprised at how much time had passed. "Yup! Be right out," I said, shoving the journal back into my backpack as I headed for the door.

"I was beginning to worry," Jenn said.

"Sorry," I said, shaking my head. "I just started thinking and lost track of time."

"About Granddaddy?"

I shrugged, "Not exactly, but yeah, in a way."

She nodded. "So you didn't hear them call your name."

"They called my name!?" I answered, snapping out of my thoughts.

"Yup," Jenn said linking her arm with mine and leading us towards the wrestling area.

"Who's next?" I asked knowing Jenn would have the answer.

"The Wyoming State Champion."

I didn't know much about him. But if he was a state champ, he was good. I just had to be better.... I had to be on my game... in the zone... no distractions... focused.... And with those thoughts, the adrenaline started pumping through my veins. "What mat number?" I asked.

"Number seven," she said giving my arm a solid squeeze.

"Seven." I repeated turning and looking into her twinkling brown eyes. "Well then, this must by my lucky day!" I said, returning her smile with a broad one of my own. We both understood what wasn't being said. The soreness in my neck from the last match was history. I was going to be wrestling on my lucky-number-seven mat, and I was feeling like there was no way I was going to lose this one.

"Let's do this!" I said, the fire in my gut growing as I headed towards my next match.

14.

Granddaddy?

"If we will be quiet and ready enough, we shall find compensation in every disappointment."
— Henry David Thoreau

I tried to steady my breathing by taking slow deep breaths. Sweat poured down my face and I swiped my arm across my brow to clear it before lining up for the 3rd and last period of my match against the Wyoming state champ. I double-checked my hands and knees, making sure they were properly placed for the down starting position. I was well ahead in points, but giving up easy points to my opponent for lining up wrong was an unacceptable sloppy mental mistake I wasn't going to make. Discipline with little things mattered because a bunch of little things done correctly could add up to a BIG accomplishment. This was my chance to win this match right here—right now!

As I stared down at my hands, my eyes suddenly focused in on how black the creases on the backs of them were. I knew why they looked like that. I always got oil on my hands when I worked at the gas station. I always washed them with the gunky gas station soap that was supposed to get rid of the oil too. But no matter how hard I scrubbed, I just couldn't get it all off of my hands. Would it ever come off? I wondered. Or was it permanently grooved into my hands the same way music and lyrics are grooved into the surface of a vinyl record—the same way our experiences are grooved into our minds and souls? A record never has to worry about remembering or forgetting, and in one respect, that's good. But a record will never play anything other than the song grooved into it—ever.

I wanted more than oil-stained hands, and even though I was technically a teenager, I was always working hard. That's why I was taking my time setting up. But now it was like time had momentarily frozen, and thoughts about my hands started to spiral in different directions. Maybe the reasons my hands still looked black even after washing them was because of the newspapers I handled every morning. Were dirty hands just part of working hard? Would people think less of me if I had a workingman's hands? It was all very strange. My opponent was waiting for me to finish setting up my hand position so he could set his starting position, so we could get back to the brawl. And yet I was daydreaming about the oil on my hands....

"Ready?" the impatient hoarse-voiced referee asked.

"What?" I responded, looking up and around trying to get my bearings.

"Ready!" he asked much louder.

This time his military-sounding tone pulled me fully back to the present. I had no idea how long I'd been daydreaming, but my mind was back in focus now. This time when I looked down at my hands, I did it quickly and efficiently, and then looked back to the referee and nodded. I was ready to get this done.

While the Wyoming State Champ set up, I looked down at my hands again, this time visualizing the first move I was going to hit. On the sound of the whistle, I was going to fire up and out like a sprinter exploding out of the starting blocks. It was a very fast and very powerful move I'd practiced over and over and over. Being able to visualize it so clearly was going to help me be a half-step faster too. In fact, I think visualizing was one of the reasons I had so much success with this stand-up wrestling move this year.

My hands still looked good, and my toes were digging into the mat in preparation for my explosion. Wait a minute! Did I... Did I see Granddaddy the first time I looked up at the referee? My head was suddenly filled with a split-second image of a man in a gray jacket and dark blue baseball cap sitting in about the third row. I didn't consciously notice him, but when I looked up the first time the referee asked me if I was ready, my unconscious mind must have seen what I didn't—Granddaddy!

I lifted my head quickly, trying to scan the crowd where I thought I'd seen him, but the referee was standing right in the middle of my line of vision. *Come on ref,* I thought. *Get out of the way!*

Tweeeep!

Before the referee was even done blowing his whistle, I was already firing up and out with my stand-up move exactly the way I'd visualized it. That's another advantage of being good at visualizing. Not only am I faster, but even being as distracted as I was, I didn't have to think about what I was going to do. I just executed my move the way I'd visualized it.

This move worked great against most wrestlers too, but this time I was wrestling a state champ who was really good, and he just as quickly trapped my ankle and prevented me from fully standing up and getting away. Instead, I fell flat on my face. I had to get out of the situation, but I took a second to look up into the stands, straining to catch another glimpse of the third row where the man with that gray jacket and dark blue baseball hat was sitting. Again, the referee was blocking my view!

I quickly pulled my mind back into the match and assessed my situation. My opponent had hold of my ankle, my leg was trapped in his iron grip, and now he was attacking my head, painfully forcing it closer and closer toward my trapped leg. His was trying to cradle me up, but I wasn't going to let him. Ohhh.... Dang! How did he get that cradle move on me! I couldn't believe I was in a cradle, and... ouch... his hold on me was starting to hurt. This was not a position I was used to. I could barely breathe and was steadily approaching panic mode as a result. What if I can't get out of this?

Instinctively, I knew it was better to fight the pain while I was still positioned on my side than it was to procrastinate and just hope it would go away. If I hesitated, he'd eventually force me onto my back and that was a much more dangerous position to be in. I was going to have to explode out of this now, and that meant finding the strength and courage to execute my next move right now.

I'm not losing this match! I decided. My move would be risky, but if I hit it quickly, there was a very good chance of getting away with it. So, instead of fighting to move away from him, I unexpectedly turned into him. That took the pressure off my head and neck while giving him a false sense of confidence. With my surprise move, I was able to quickly grab onto one of his legs with both of my hands. I was buried underneath him now, and doubled up on his leg in a position that diminished the controlling and painful pressure he was applying to my head.

My position was slowly improving, and I could feel his frustration growing. He'd thought he had me, but now he was realizing that he didn't. Next, I forced my head to slide out from underneath his weight by moving it in a half-moon arc—sweeping down, across, and up again to the side of him. On the upward swing of this technique, I powerfully drove my head up his body toward the stadium lights. At the same time, I arched my back as hard as I could—like a gymnast hitting a back flip. I could hear him grunting as I fully stretched myself and inhaled deeply.

It worked! His grip on me was broken, and his body lifted up and off the mat. Now he was flying in an out-of-control arcing spiral pattern. I couldn't see him because I was still finishing my move. I knew exactly where he was though, and deftly sank in a blind half nelson wrestling hold on him. My acrobatic throw had worked, and now he was in even bigger trouble as we crash landed on the mat with me on top and him on the bottom lying slightly on his side and slightly on his back.

Wow! He was really good! Most of my opponents would have fallen directly onto their backs from this move, but he'd done some maneuvering of his own while he was in the air, and managed to land partially on his side rather than fully on his back. He was certainly an impressive wrestler! However, his superb ability and tactical maneuvers weren't going to be enough today. His airborne maneuver had only slightly improved his position and we both knew it. I had a deep half nelson in on him and could see the fear in his eyes. I gritted my teeth and felt a fresh surge of adrenaline starting to pump through my veins. I had him right where I wanted him. He would not escape. He was mine now, and I went in for the kill.

I drove into him with everything I had, further spiraling him from his side to his back while simultaneously capturing one of his legs. Now I had him totally trapped, upside down and tightly wrapped up and twisted like a giant pretzel, squeezing the life out of him with all of my might.

I knew it was rare to pin a state champ wrestler, but I was beginning to believe that this might turn out to be one of those rare times. My heart was pounding, and my muscles were filing with blood, causing them to bulge triumphantly. As my confidence continued to build, I could feel my opponent's strength and resolve slipping away.

SLAP! Tweeeep!

I'd done it! I'd actually done it! I pinned the state champ from Wyoming, and now I was one step closer to the All-American rounds! I practically jumped to my feet and quickly started looking around for Granddaddy. The referee made this difficult by re-directing me back to the center for the after-match shaking-hands ritual. I was still trying to look through the audience, but it was impossible to make out anyone's face with everybody jumping up and down and hooting and hollering over the series of amazing moves I'd used to win my match. My opponent and I had put on one heck of a good fight, and this was the audience's way of letting us know how much they appreciated what we'd done.

When we were both standing in the center of the wrestling mat we shook hands. He had been an excellent adversary and I was impressed with his composure. Even after the beat-down I'd just given him, his handshake was strong and confident. The referee then took hold of my wrist and raised my arm high in victory. The crowd responded with an even louder roar while the defeated state champ walked back to his coach.

After the referee let go of my arm and walked away to record my victory, I was finally able to get a good look into the third row of the bleachers. I saw the man I was looking for, but my heart sank as soon as I focused on his face. It wasn't Granddaddy, so I turned away and walked towards my coach, the thrill of the victory draining out of me with each step.

Coach was clapping and had a big smile on his face. "Hey! Dakota!" he bellowed above the cheers for another wrestler who'd just won his match. "That was a huge match! It was a good win too. You looked good. Tough start in the third period, but you worked it out. Well done. How do you feel?

"I'm okay," I said, looking past him to Jenn. She had a huge smile on her face and happy tears in her eyes. "Thanks Coach," I said before picking up my stuff and walking to where Jenn was standing. She let me wrap my arms around her and returned the hug completely ignoring how sweaty I was. When we let go of each other, she looked into my face.

"What's wrong?" she asked, her expression filled with concern.

"I thought I saw Granddaddy."

"Where?" she asked, quickly looking around. "Is he here? Did he leave?"

"It wasn't him. I saw a hat that looked like the one that Granddaddy had worn that day and... well... it wasn't him." I looked down, determined not to give into the tears of disappointment prickling at the back of eyes.

"I'm sorry Dakota. That sucks," she said, linking one of her arms through mine. "Good win though. You were very impressive. I'm kinda proud of you."

That got a smile out of me, but I shook my head. "I don't know Jenn. It's so strange. I just scored one of the biggest victories of my life and all I can feel is how disappointed I am that Granddaddy wasn't here to see it. And I know that's wrong because you're here with me. Heck, even my mom's here."

"I get it," she said." And I don't think it's wrong either." Her big brown eyes searched mine, and we both smiled, both knowing what she was going to say next.

"I know," I said with a small chuckle, asking the question before she could. "What would Granddaddy have to say about this situation? That's one of the things I love about you Jenn. You say what has to be said."

A Sprint to the Top

15.

Taking a Time Out

"While you feel compelled to charge forward it's often a gentle step back that will reveal to you where you are and what you truly seek."

— Rasheed Ogunlaru

I didn't have time to answer her because my mom came up to us and congratulated me on the match.

"I had no idea wrestling could be so exciting. But it looks like it hurts too," she said with a look of concern. "How do you keep doing it match after match?"

I laughed. "Yeah, it can definitely hurt, but it never seems to hurt quite as much when you win as it does when you lose. Don't worry Mom, I'm fine."

"Okay," she said. "I'll be back for the next match. It's the last one right? If you win this one you'll be an All-American?"

"I will. Then I'll be wrestling my way through the All-Americans," I said with a confident smile.

"Good," she said pulling her book out of her purse. "See you in a while."

I headed to the locker room for some quiet time, but I was too distracted with thinking that I'd seen Granddaddy to focus. After a while, I gave up and went to find Jenn.

She smiled when she saw me. "What's up?" she asked.

"I couldn't concentrate, so I came out here instead."

"Are you thinking about the match?"

"I wish. I need to. I need to get my focus back on track.

"Okay," she started, "Let's talk it out. What's the plan?"

I couldn't think what she meant for a few seconds. Then I got it. She was asking about the plan I had in place for today. I always had a plan. I remember Granddaddy talking about the difference between people who have plans and those who don't. People who don't make plans are destined to live their lives at the mercy of other people's plans. Planning may take time and effort, but I was determined not to be at anyone else's mercy.

My strategy was to always break big plans down into little plans. Little plans were things like deciding how I was going to spend my time. It wasn't like I planned out every second, but if I knew I had to study, I'd plan time for it. This strategy continued to pay off big—especially with wrestling. I'd spent a lot of time breaking big moves down into a series of smaller movements, and got so good at them that I could execute them like they were second nature. Now when I step on the mat, I'm better and quicker at deciding what to do next, like in my last match. The great part about doing things this way was that every time I got all those little plans worked out, the big ones seemed to fall right into place too.

Today, I was one win away from accomplishing one of my big plans. Winning the next match wouldn't just make me an All-American, it would pretty much guarantee a wrestling scholarship too. What a relief that was going to be! I knew there were ways to borrow money for school, and I might still have to borrow some, but at least I'd be able to go to a good college and get a good education. Heck, Granddaddy had five degrees, and two of them were doctorates! I had a lot of catching up to do.

Jenn nudged my shoulder with hers. "The plan?" she prompted.

I tried to shake myself out of my thoughts. "Right... the plan.

The plan for today is to execute."

When I didn't say anything else, she added, "So.... So far so good?"

I nodded, looking around the arena.

"Hey... Dakota... What's up? I usually can't get you to stop talking when you start talking about a plan."

"I know," I said shaking my head. "It's crazy Jenn, but seeing that hat just brought it all back. It was like he was here again."

Jenn's eyebrows rose ever so slightly. "You came out here so you could be on the look-out for him, didn't you."

Was she right? It took me about half-a-second to realize she was. "I didn't realize it until you said it, but you're right. I wanted to be out here—."

"Just in case Granddaddy was here?"

I nodded again.

"I can see why. I've been thinking about him too. He said he was always watching over you. And... well... we never actually saw his body at his funeral."

"No, we didn't. But you know what's even worse than that?" I added, feeling a pained expression take over my face.

Jenn shook her head.

"I wish I'd seen it. And I know how horrible that sounds. Wishing I'd seen his body is like wishing he was dead and I hate myself for thinking that. But then something like what just happened here happens, and I hate that too. I don't know how I'm supposed to think. And then, we have disturbing thought number three," I said holding up three fingers for emphasis. "If Granddaddy was here, he could help me figure out what I'm supposed to think about him being dead!" I closed my eyes and rubbed my temples as if that might help me get rid of some of the loss, confusion, and straight-up self-pity I was feeling.

Jenn sighed. "I hear what you're saying, but you're forgetting about interesting thought number four."

I tipped my head up to meet her eyes.

"You're leaving out the part about what it means if he's not dead—if he really is still alive. People don't fake their deaths for no reason. If he faked his death, it must have been for one heck of a reason. And forgive me for saying this, but it probably wasn't because he didn't want to see you again."

As usual, Jenn had pushed the right button, and I laughed at myself. "You're right.... And remember all the soldiers at his funeral?"

"I do. And you learned he was still active military that day too. You didn't know that before."

"Yeah. Grandma said he was a Colonel."

"So maybe the question we should be asking is, if Granddaddy did fake his own death, what was the reason?"

I sat up straight at that thought. "You're right. We didn't talk about that possibility after the funeral. Everything had felt so real that I guess I just accepted the fact he really was dead. If he's still alive, maybe he's doing something really important. Maybe he's a spy?" I volunteered with a hopeful smile.

Jenn shrugged. "Maybe. I don't know if it matters what he's doing. And... it kinda brings us right back to where we started."

I was looking around again, nodding in agreement with what she'd said. And then I jumped to my feet. "There's that hat again," I said pointing to the other side of the arena. "Maybe I was looking at the wrong guy before!"

"Are you sure that isn't the same guy you saw?" Jenn asked.

"I can't tell from here."

"Well, come on. Let's go see."

She took my hand and we moved as quickly as we could around the arena. I could see the hat clearly now, and it was definitely the same kind of hat Granddaddy had been wearing that day. But when we got close enough to get a good look, my heart sank even lower than it had 45 minutes ago. The man wearing it didn't even remotely look like Granddaddy.

Jenn took one look at my face and pulled me through one of the arena exit doors. When we were outside, we walked to an empty bench and sat on the cold steel.

"Okay. It wasn't him," she said. "But that doesn't mean he's dead. He could still be alive. I mean... think about it. If he's still alive, and he is working with the military, it's probably not here. Nothing ever happens here."

I nodded working through the logic of what Jenn was saying.

"You're right. If he's working with the military, he might be undercover. And if he's undercover, it couldn't be here because too many people know him... and that means... I can stop looking for him."

"I agree."

I looked at Jenn. "Do you think I'll ever see him again?"

She shrugged.

"Yeah, I don't know either. I think it will be easier to think about him this way though... like maybe he's working undercover for the government. It's better than thinking about him being dead.... Ugh... my head's a mess right now. I've got to get my brain back into wrestling. I've got the match of my life coming up in," I said, pushing a button on Jenn's cell phone to check the time. "Holy smoke! I gotta go!"

A Sprint to the Top

16.

Lessons for Life

"Mistakes are part of being human. Appreciate your mistakes for what they are, precious life lessons that can only be learned the hard way."

— Al Franken

As soon as Coach and I locked eyes, he looked at his watch and then at me. "Cutting it kind of close kid," he said, his tone part anger, part relief.

"I'm sorry Coach. I was—"

"Stop," he said holding up one hand. "It almost sounds like you're about to give me an excuse, and you know how I feel about excuses."

I nodded. I did know how he felt about them. As far as Coach was concerned, there wasn't room for excuses in sports. I can't even count the times he'd said: "When you put your best effort into something, you never have to make excuses for the result. With your best efforts in play, even a bad result can be dealt with. Having an excuse is like preparing for failure. Besides, there isn't any excuse on earth that can change the result after the fact."

I'd read about excuses in the journal Granddaddy had left me too. Granddaddy wrote that people use excuses to lessen the impact of the things they've done, as if coming up with a good enough excuse or reason could somehow make a bad result "okay." He also wrote that people never seemed to make excuses when they succeeded.

Both Granddaddy and Coach were right. Now when I hear someone making excuses for when things don't work out the way they wanted them to, it sticks out like a sore thumb. If someone doesn't get a good grade, or does poorly in competition, it's like they've got a whole bunch of excuses lined up and ready to go. But if they do good, then they're happy to take all the credit and praise they can get.

Coach put a steady hand on my shoulder, looked me straight in the eye, and talked as if we were the only two people in the gymnasium. "Have you been paying attention to what's going on in this tournament?" he asked, his voice grizzly and deep and yet somehow reassuring.

"Yes." I responded weakly, forcing myself to look him straight in the eye when I said it—because that's the only way you should ever look at anyone. I noticed that sweat had beaded up on his forehead, and it was weird seeing this mammoth man look so nervous. He was a former heavyweight college wrestling champ, and a former professional football player, and I didn't think there was anything that could make him nervous. And besides, I was the one who was supposed to be nervous, not him.

"Good... but listen. I know there's a lot riding on this next match. Win this match, and your next match will be in the All-American rounds. And I know how exciting that is to think about, but sometimes things can get moving so fast that it's hard to stay focused right where you are. And right now, I can tell by the look on your face that your head's not in this. If you go into this next match like this, your chance to win might come and go in the blink of an eye.

"Every competitor who's made it this far is a force to be reckoned with, and every one of them wants to win just as much as you do. And sometimes, it comes down to what you can endure just as much as it does to what you can do. You've already been through some tough rounds. Remember that your next opponent is determined to push you just as hard as you're determined to push him.

"One of your biggest advantages is that you know this can happen. You know that you might end up feeling exhausted, or hurting, or that your opponent might be close to choking the heck out of you during this match. But you also know that if you stay focused, and trust in all the hard work you've been putting in, then you won't be in the position of looking for excuses to give up. You'll be figuring out how to fight so you can do what you came here to do. And that's all any man can ask of himself. Are you ready to stay focused and bring everything you know how to do to that mat so you can do what you came here to do?"

"Yes Coach!" I yelled in response, feeling the competitor in me surging to life.

"Good! Then let's do this!" Coach thundered in his larger-than-life Zeus-like voice that went hand in hand with his size and stature.

We descended the stairs down into the restricted area like warriors ready to do battle. As soon as we stepped onto the floor, I heard my name being called out to wrestle the Montana State Champ. My heart started to pound and I could feel my palms getting sweaty. But if there was one thing I'd learned over the years of combat competitions, it was that a little nervous energy was a good thing. Early on, Coach taught me that nervous energy was a part of competing, and that it could either fuel my fire, or put it out. The choice was mine to make.

Now I thought of my pre-match nerves as an extra boost of energy—an additional power source that could help me be a bit sharper and perform a bit better. I'd learned how to recognize this energy, take charge of it, and use it, whether it was to wrestle a state champ, run with the football, or read in front of the class at school. I believed this was how it probably went with most things in life too—you got better at doing something the more often you did it. Learning how to master my nervous energy now, meant I'd be able to use it to my advantage in the future too.

It wasn't easy during those early days of competition though. When I first started wrestling, as soon as my palms started getting sweaty I started to freak out inside. What if I wasn't good enough? What if my opponent was better than me? What if I lost? I didn't want to be a "loser," and back then I hated all those wild butterflies messing with my belly before every match. It was like they were reminding me of everything that could go wrong, and all the chaos they created in my stomach made it hard for me to concentrate.

Somehow Coach had known what was going on in my head and pointed out that those butterflies weren't likely to ever go away, so I might as well figure out how to use them to my advantage. And he was right. Even after all my experience in the combat sport of wrestling, my palms still got sweaty before every match. In truth, I didn't know how anyone could go into any kind of competition without being at least a little bit nervous— especially when there were people watching you.

Now that I was older, wiser, and more experienced, I knew the butterflies were going to be there, and kind of looked forward to their presence. Now I imagined them flying in the same kind of strategic wedge formation Granddaddy's WWII fighter squadron probably used during the war. My butterflies weren't about fear anymore, and it was kind of nice to have a squadron of killer butterflies on my side, especially when they've been commanded to accept nothing less than total victory! Now they remind me to get excited about what was coming up. They remind me that I'd done a good job of preparing for battle, and that I was ready to bring my best to the challenge in front of me so I could achieve my goal. My butterflies were definitely bad news for my opponents!

As I finished my quick warm-up, I could see my opponent squeezing in a last minute warm-up of his own.

Coach gave me one last reassuring glare. "You ready!?" he asked with the same intensity he always had when one of his wrestlers was ready to step onto the mat. To my ears, it was like a battle cry.

"Ready," I answered decisively before turning towards the arena and my next opponent.

Taking our cue from the referee, my opponent and I walked towards the center of the wrestling mat, following the pre-wrestling protocol of shaking hands. As I stood across from him, I sized him up. He looked brawny and resilient, but like Coach said, at this level we were all tough and worthy opponents. So it didn't matter what he looked like. Regardless of how tough of an opponent he was going to be, when the dust from this rumble settled, only one of us would continue on to the All-American rounds, and I had every intention of being that one! And in that instant, I visualized my butterflies falling into formation, and welcomed the rush of adrenaline that started pumping through my veins. I was definitely ready for combat!

We released our handshake, and the referee blew the whistle while leaping out of the way. We both charged like rams and collided in the center of the wrestling mat. We locked "horns" and start pushing and shoving each other, testing out each other's toughness and sheer physical strength. Within a few moments, I knew this guy was definitely a worthy opponent, and for a split second, I let my mind take in how much I loved being here. Goose bumps ran down my back, and I shivered with pride as my mind instantly snapped back into focus.

I worked vigorously for inside control. That would give me a slight advantage in getting past his first line of defense—his arms. If I could do that, I'd be able to attack his control center—his body. After some serious pushing, shoving, pulling, and moving around in all different directions, I gained inside control, and decided it was time to outfox and out-maneuver Montana's state champ.

I used my explosive speed to quickly drop my body level and move in on his legs using a penetration step wrestling technique. The maneuver allowed me to use a "high C" technique, aka a "high crotch" wrestling move. I heard the crowd roaring, but was so focused, the noise sounded muffled.

With the "high C," I was now controlling the core of his body so he couldn't move or easily get away from my grip. I hadn't scored any points yet, but it sure looked good for me right now, and it sure looked bad for him.

He fought back like I expected him to, squirming with all his might to create space between us by getting his hips back. If he succeeded in creating enough space, he'd be in a stronger position, and not as vulnerable to giving up valuable points. While he was trying to drive his hips back (or sprawling as we call it in wrestling) he simultaneously threw a vicious crossface move, driving the hard bony section of his forearm across my nose.

This crossface pressure was very uncomfortable. Worse than that, it forced my head back. In wrestling, there's a saying that where the head goes the body must follow, so this was bad for me. Not only did his counter move hurt like heck, it was beginning to create a little bit of space between us which made it harder and harder for me to control him. Maybe I wouldn't be scoring points here after all.

This guy had one of the boniest forearms I'd ever encountered! But that was just part of the battle. That was part of the test. If I wanted to win this match, I had to fight through the pain. So I focused my will, and using all of my body's momentum, I drove up and into his crossface in spite of the additional pain I was taking on by doing it. My driving force caused him to become more defensive, and even more aggressive, which meant even more pain for me. I smiled through it though, because that was exactly what I wanted him to do!

Like clockwork, in a perfectly orchestrated movement, I

quickly stopped driving into him and dropped the height of my body level again. He hadn't expected me to take away the resistance that had been supporting the force of his body's weight against mine. His crossface hold slipped off my face, and his body momentarily fell over me. Now I was temporarily supporting his body weight, except that it was on my shoulders instead of my head.

I immediately took full advantage of my superior position. With both of my knees still on the mat, I proceeded to step up and place my left foot on the mat next to him while leaving my right knee on the mat under him as support. Simultaneously, I lifted my head up really high. Next, I pivoted on my right knee and swung my body in a semi-circle—like a gate door swinging on its hinges. The maneuver robbed my opponent of the temporary support of my right shoulder, and now he was crashing down onto the mat like a ton of bricks. While he was falling, I quickly finished my spiral move and landed safely, down low behind him. I captured one of his ankles, and before he could recover, I quickly grabbed and trapped his other ankle too.

My opponent was a strong competitor though, and he tried to save himself by reaching back and trying to push my head to the mat. If he could pin my head, he could slow me down and buy himself some time to figure out how to get out of the mess of trouble he was in. He probably would have been better off trying to trap my head by sitting on it, but he didn't. Instead he stuck with his current counter move. It slowed me down and I had to struggle some, but his attempt just wasn't enough to stop a guy like me. Eventually, I worked my head free and worked my way up from his trapped ankles to his torso and back. Now I was in full control, forcing his body down flat on the big red wrestling mat, driving him deeper and deeper into the red zone.

The referee awarded the first two points of the match to me, and none for him. Now I felt like I had command over the tone and tempo of our match. Everything continued to go well for me, and I felt like the win was within my sights. He was a worthy adversary though, and in the second period, he almost scored a takedown move of his own. Unfortunately for him, he came up short when we both fell out of bounds.

At the start of the third period my opponent got to pick his starting position, and he chose top. He hadn't had that option yet because I'd been too good to allow that to happen. But now I didn't have a choice. I felt okay about it though. I was definitely getting tired, but I also had a commanding 10-4 lead.

I looked in Coach's direction and could see that he was really fired up. He was yelling in my direction, but I couldn't make out what he was saying over the roar of the crowd. I was paying attention to the referee too, waiting for his signal to set my down position for the start. When I got the signal, I started setting my down position, and had one of those moments of pure focus. Suddenly I was able to pull Coach's voice in front of all the background noise.

"You got this kid! Be smart! Be careful! He picked top for a reason! Stay off your back! He can't beat you outright! But he can pin you! Stay off your back! Do not get pinned! You hear me? Do not get pinned!" Coach's rapid-fire voice commanded.

I listened, letting every word sink in. I'd heard Coach yell before—especially when I was just getting started as a wrestler. But... don't get pinned? I had no intention of getting pinned. I was a seasoned warrior. I'd already established that I was a better wrestler than my opponent and we both knew it. I owned him, and as soon as that whistle blew, I was going to escape from the bottom so fast he wouldn't even know what happened. Then I was going to score some more points on my way to victory. Heck, I thought with a grin, maybe I'll even pin him.

Tweeeep!

I hit my stand-up move with blazing speed. But something

strange happened this time too. He stopped it! I was definitely surprised, but not deterred—and certainly not worried. I just needed to start working for a rock-solid bottom base position, get wrist control, and then hit my slower, steadier, power stand-up move. It would take a little longer than I had anticipated, but I would be up and out and smoothly flying home to a nice victory parade in no time at all.

The problem was that this guy was good from the top wrestling position. He was keeping me off balance so I couldn't get a rock-solid bottom base position to successfully work from. His rapid movements and maneuvers were a bit of a surprise too. He was relentlessly hitting me with ankle and arm attacks, as well as spiral riding breakdowns, and leg riding. *Did he just use a variation of the old-fashion crab ride? Where did he learn that move? And where did he get all this new-found energy from?*

He had just hit a flurry of moves with a level of vigor, energy, and confidence I hadn't seen from him so far, and now I was remembering what Coach had said, "There's a reason he chose top!" Maybe the top wrestling position was his specialty. Maybe this was how he wore his opponents down. He overwhelmed them with a bunch of rapid fire moves and then pinned them. Maybe this was part of *his* plan—to get on top and then wear me down until he defeated me.

Oh no! He had one of my arms trapped now—really trapped. *Okay.... No problem.... Relax.... Breathe.... Don't panic.... It's okay.... I'm a warrior and I'm being challenged.* Like with his earlier crossface move, the hold he had on me was applying a very painful force that was going to be too hard to endure for much longer.

This is bad. I thought. *He's got real leverage on me, and dang, it feels like my arm is about to pop out of my shoulder socket! If that happens, that's it. No college will even talk to me if I ruin my shoulder. Think Dakota! Think!*

Time can be so strange sometimes. Sometimes an hour flashes by in the blink of an eye, and sometimes seconds seem to last forever. Right now, I was in seconds-lasting-forever time, and what I needed to do was to take my attention off the excruciating pain I was experiencing, and put it back into finding a way out of my painful predicament. I didn't have a lot of options though, and then my mind flashed on a move—a crazy move. It wasn't a move I'd ever really practiced because I never visualized myself getting trapped like this. I was pretty sure I could execute it, and yes, it was taking a chance, but it might work. So far, I'd been handling this guy pretty easily. And worst case scenario, even if the move didn't work out the way I hoped it would, it was better than doing nothing and letting this guy rip my shoulder out. There was just too much riding on this match to let that happen without a fight!

If I quickly changed the direction of my resistance by rolling with his pressure and then quickly sitting up, I should be able to use his momentum against him and maybe even put him on his back. I didn't know if the move would work because I'd never tried it before. I couldn't even remember the last time I'd been this vulnerable in a match. But if it did work, he'd be on his back looking up at the lights and I'd end up winning by pin.

Okay. Ready... Set... Go...! I hit the roll, but somehow, he shifted his bodyweight in a way I hadn't anticipated, and now I was on my back with him on top of me in a commanding position. I wasn't completely down yet, but he was cutting off my air, and I had a few more "forever" seconds to realize that in some ways, our strengths are also our weaknesses.

Why hadn't I spent just as much time working on defensive moves as I had on all my power moves? The answer to that question was easy. I'd never really had to. I'd spent so much time being "better" than everyone else that I'd never even considered the possibility that my best might not be enough. And yet here I was, on my back, with my opponent patiently and persistently robbing me of my oxygen. I could feel the drive to fight back seeping out of me, and for the first time, I realized I could lose this match even though I was the better wrestler. That must have been what Coach was trying to tell me: "He can't beat you outright! But he can pin you!"

I should have fought smarter from my bottom base position instead of trying to hit that roll-through move. Rolls weren't really my thing, and truth be told, I was never any good at them. They always seemed too defensive or too passive for me. I was the kind of guy who wanted to look my opponent in the eye and stand toe to toe with him. I should have stuck to my game plan and not have let myself be distracted by what he was doing. Instead, I'd reacted, and he'd been able to take advantage of it. I should have remembered Coach's number one rule too: Respect all, fear none. I should have had more respect for this state champ's abilities.

I don't know how long I was on my back, but things weren't getting any better, and the thought of just putting my shoulders down on the mat so I could instantly get out of this painful situation started running through my mind. There were two very long minutes left in the round. Could I last that long without passing out and ending up getting pinned anyway? I could barely breathe now, and desperately needed air. *Fight!* my inner voice screamed, and I knew I had do to something. If I couldn't find a way to stay in this fight, in a time and place I'd fought so hard to get to, how could I count on myself to do what had to be done in the future?

No! I won't give up! I won't give in! I have to fight this! I pulled together the strength I'd built up from hundreds of workouts and mentally linked it to my squadron of adrenaline-pumped butterflies for one last Herculean effort to explode up and out upon command.

KABOOM!!! I was out! I was off my back and back to my belly again. I could hear the crowd cheering my gutsy move, but I also heard the referee award my opponent three back-exposure points, and now the score was 10-7. I was still winning, but between my time on my back, and the effort it just took to get out, I was wiped out and wondered if I had enough strength and composure to get through the rest of the match. My opponent had no intention of letting me have any time to do anything though, and commenced with another barrage of offensive attacks. I knew that if I could just fend him off long enough to catch my breath, I could try to hit my stand-up move and get up, out, and away from him.

Crap! How did he manage to trap my arm—again!—and with the same move as before! I couldn't find anything to work with and felt myself going over on my back... and in slow motion, the realization that maybe my best wasn't good enough threatened to take over my mind. Was this really how this was going to end?

Over the noise of the crowd, my brain picked out Coach's voice shouting out the same thing over and over.

"DO WHAT YOU CAME HERE TO DO! DO WHAT YOU CAME HERE TO DO!"

His voice sounded harsh, but it reminded me what my goal for today was. To win! I had made a commitment to do what I had to do, every round, to win. Of course, knowing that didn't change my current problem, which was that I was really close to getting pinned. I'd already executed the only move I could think of and it hadn't worked. Laying there on my back until the end of the round wasn't going to work either though. Even if I managed to stay strong enough to not let him pin me, he'd still get three points for exposing my back to the mat, and then the match would be tied at 10-10. That would mean overtime, and I doubted I could handle another round. For one thing, I'd never had to wrestle in overtime. For another, I wasn't sure how well I'd do against an opponent who was clearly smelling blood in the water. This was definitely a new experience for me.

"DO WHAT YOU CAME HERE TO DO! DO WHAT YOU CAME HERE TO DO!"

Was that Jenn yelling? I was sure it was her and immediately remembered her asking me what the plan for today was. I'd answered her with one word: Execute. Except that right now it was more like I was being executed than doing any executing. Granddaddy has said that no man succeeds in a vacuum, and he'd been right. In the midst of all the pain and stress I was feeling about the possibility of failing, I'd forgotten to do what I came here to do, and both Jenn and Coach were doing everything they could to remind me.

I gritted my teeth, and I got mad. I was determined not to go down like this. I was going to do something. I was going to take action! I growled, and then I yelled and exploded with a ferocity rarely seen in high school sports. I threw my opponent off me as we both launch into the air. And somehow, during my volcanic eruption, I managed to fly right up and land on my feet.

I heard the referee give my opponent three offensive back exposure points. That tied the match at 10-10 until the referee gave me one point for my defensive escape, and once again I had a winning lead at 11-10 with less than thirty seconds left in the match. I was beyond exhausted, and briefly thought about how nice it would be to take a nap right about now, but instead, I just about smiled because I was right where I wanted to be, standing toe-to-toe with a worthy opponent.

Unfortunately, because I was so tired now, when I looked at my opponent this time, I saw three of him. Yup, three of him, and I was comically wondering how I was supposed to attack a trio of Montana State Wrestling Champs. I couldn't remember Coach ever teaching us a strategy for taking on multiple opponents.

I briefly considered letting the clock run out by stalling and doing everything I could to stay out of my opponent's reach. But if I did that, the referee was sure to penalize me by giving my opponent a point. Then the match would be tied, and that would mean overtime. Besides, those kinds of tactics weren't my style. I wasn't a counter-puncher. I was a take-charge person, and when it came to doing what I came here to do, that meant executing.

My best defense had always been a strong offense. That was how I'd been able to keep my opponents at bay in the past, and that meant I needed to keep attacking to keep him off balance. I couldn't risk giving him another chance to attack me and work his moves. I couldn't rely on defensive moves I'd never practiced either. The only real option was to trust my instincts and go with an offensive attack.

The good news was that he had to be tired too. I blinked my eyes hard, trying to reduce the number of opponents down to one, and focused my mind with one command: Execute. We were going to wrestle to the end, so I stepped toward the trio of Montana State Wrestling champs to do the thing my instincts were telling me to do—attack the guy in the middle. Without stopping to think about it, I immediately and aggressively shot in on the legs of the one in the middle before he had time to react and adjust his double-leg takedown defenses. When I made contact, I was relieved to know I had attacked the right one!

I was in deep on him now, and could feel his legs securely trapped within the tight grasp of my arms as I maneuvered for a takedown. He didn't seem to be putting up the kind of fight I thought he would, but there was no time to think about that. It was time to use the thimble-full of adrenalin I'd managed to muster up. I lifted and spiraled him like a tornado down to the mat, and secured the takedown. *Yes!* I shouted inwardly.

The score was now 13-10 with me firmly in charge. I threw my legs in on my opponent to leg ride him, while simultaneously hooking both of my arms under his armpits, wrapping my hands up and on his shoulders to ride him like a turtle's shell for the last few seconds of the match. He tried to shake me off, but it was useless. I was on him tight and I wasn't going anywhere except for a cruise down victory lane. *Come on buzzer....!*

When the buzzer finally went off, I jumped up and staggered around trying to regain my strength and balance. My vision started to clear and by the time I was standing in the center of the mat there were only two newly defeated Montana State Wrestling Champs waiting to shake my hand. With laser-like focus, I made my decision and extended my hand to one of them. I'd picked the right one, and we shook, like the honorable men we both were.

"Great job!" he said.

I nodded my head in acknowledgement, and then the referee grabbed my wrist and raised my arm high in victory while saying, "Great job, Kiddo! Way to hang tough!"

I wanted to say something back, but I was just too physically tired to speak out loud. In my head though, I was being all cocky with myself. *Hey, I just did what I came here to do.*

A Sprint to the Top

17.

Confidence

"Each time we face our fear, we gain strength, courage and confidence in the doing."

— Theodore Roosevelt

Coach put his fist out and I bumped it. "Congrats kid. You're an All-American! Good work," he said while giving me the once over. "You okay?"

I nodded. "Yeah, I'm okay," I said, trying to calm my breathing. "That was... ah...."

Coach nodded. "Yeah it was. But you stuck with it. You took some chances out there too. But better than that, you committed to every move. You can be proud of the work you did out there."

"Thanks Coach. I feel pretty good about it," I said, trying to convince myself that I really did feel that way. "But right now—"

"I get it," Coach said looking over his shoulder and spotting Jenn. "Go do what you gotta do."

Jenn was waiting for me with a big smile on her face. In my mind, I imagined myself doing a perfect jock-jog to where she was standing, but didn't trust my rubber legs to cooperate. Instead, I walked slowly, feeling as though every muscle in my body had been stretched to its limit.

"You did it Dakota!" she said wrapping her arms around me. "I knew you could," she added, pulling back and looking into my eyes. "I knew you would... but I know it was tough too. You okay?"

That was a question I was being asked more often than I was

used to. Most of the time my wins were right on target and earned without too much effort. This one had been very different though. I was thrilled I'd won, but at the moment, my body didn't feel good at all. I ached, and I was still shaking. As usual, Jenn read my mind.

"You need to regroup, so go. I'll be here," she said.

Nodding my head because I was too tired to even speak, I headed to the locker room. Inside, I turned to the right instead of the left and made my way to the last aisle of lockers. Most people would be turning left towards the showers, so no one was likely to come this way, and I stretched out on the bench between the two rows of lockers, grateful to let my neck and spine relax.

A short while later, I heard the locker room door creak open and held my breath, slowly letting it out as the footsteps headed towards the showers. Every part of my body hurt. That wasn't new... I'd been in pain after a match before. Most of the time whatever pain I'd felt had been balanced out by how good I felt about the win. I knew I should have been feeling great right now too. I'd reached the All-American Rounds. Why wasn't I jumping up and down for joy—aside from the fact that my body still wasn't in the mood for jumping yet.

I started replaying the match over in my head, trying to recapture that moment when I knew I'd won, searching for that feeling of excitement and exhilaration that usually came with it. But my thoughts were interrupted by something I never expected. Whoever was in the shower was crying now. Not a little bit either. He was really crying and I could hear every gasp and choke of it. It was the kind of crying people do in private.

It hurt to hear too, because it didn't sound like this guy was crying because he'd won. He was crying because he'd lost. Heck, he could have been the guy I just beat for all I knew. And suddenly I knew why I wasn't excited about winning. I'd been so close to losing—so freakin' close. I'd won, but my body hurt, and I was worried about getting through the next round. That thought pissed me off because there were seven other guys out there ready to go another round, and they were probably just as tired and achy as I was at this point. Why was I being such a baby about it!

Suck it up! I thought. *You're better than this! This is what you've worked for! You got this!* But they were all just words. This was a different level of competition than I'd ever experienced, and the guys who were left might all be able to beat me. Granted, I didn't have to fight every one of them, but what if my next opponent was better than me, or wasn't as tired as I was? What if my next opponent was fitter than I was? Or stronger... or smarter? Would I be the one crying in the shower after the next match?

I sat up. This was uncharted territory for me and I wasn't sure what to think or do. Sitting around listening to this guy's despair wasn't doing me any favors though, so I got up and headed out of the locker room, careful to not let the door squeak on the way out.

Jenn was right where I knew she'd be.

"Hey," I said.

"Hey," she said with a puzzled look. "You doing okay?"

I shrugged and nodded.

"You know I'm here for you, right?" she asked.

"Of course," I replied, trying to look relaxed.

"Good. Because I think you're thinking about that last match, and I think you need to talk to your coach."

I shook my head. Not because I didn't want to talk to Coach, but because I wasn't the kind of guy who needed a coach to hold my hand. I was the kind of guy who always worked it out and didn't need that kind of help.

"Yeah, I know, you're a "free agent" when it comes to coaching," Jenn said, "but I bet you'd talk to Granddaddy if he was here. And I know your coach isn't Granddaddy, but still, you always say he's a great coach. We can talk if you want, but this feels like a competitive guy thing to me."

I looked at her, and mustered up a half-smile. "Another reason why you're the best," I said. "Thanks," I added before turning and heading towards Coach. He saw me heading towards him, and I saw him giving the clock a quick look, registering the fact that my next match wasn't until 20 minutes from now.

"What's up," he asked, giving me the once over.

I shrugged.

"That was a tough match."

I nodded.

"Tough enough to have you worrying about your next match instead of thinking about it," he said.

I nodded and sighed, relieved that I didn't have to straight-up confess my problem.

"Well, let me start with something you already know. The competition at this level is tougher than you're used to. It's even tougher for you because you're a better wrestler than 90% of the other guys here, which means you're coming up against stuff you haven't had any experience with before. Think about it... how many times do you think you've been pushed to the absolute limit?"

If Coach had asked me that question yesterday, I could have probably listed a few matches, but now I knew those matches were not like the one I'd just eked out. I hadn't ever been pushed like that. That match had pushed me beyond limits I didn't even know I had. The win had been different too—and difficult.

Coach went on, "When winning comes easy, like it has for you, your body and mind get used to doing what needs to be done. But there are some situation's you just can't prepare for until you experience them. You're one of the most mentally tough competitors I've ever worked with, but all the toughness and preparation in the world can't prepare you for that first real challenge to your inner belief in your ability to get the job done.

When winning is easy, there's no self-doubt about your ability to get the job done."

Coach rubbed his chin. "I saw a look in your eyes at one point during the match that had me worried, but you muscled your way through whatever it was you were thinking about and won the match."

"It was weird," I started, still trying to work it out in my mind. "I felt like I knew what was happening the whole time. I knew what I had to do too. But it was different because he was different, but... I don't know," I said, still struggling to understand what was wrong.

"Most of the time, the limits you deal with are off the mat—like when you're upping your workouts in the gym to get stronger. But you're right. That last match was different. You had to break through a different kind of limit. You did a hell of a job getting through it too, and you should be proud of that. You didn't give up. But now you have doubts and you're nervous that you might have to do the exact same thing in your next match, and you're not sure if you can do it again, because you're not exactly sure how you did it in the last match."

As crazy as it was, I felt a huge wave of relief wash over me because Coach had nailed it. He had used a different word, calling it doubt, but that's what it was. Then I was almost sick to my stomach because even I knew that doubt was just a nice word for fear. The only time anyone doubts something is when they don't have confidence in what they believe. Did that mean I'd lost my confidence too?

"A match like that can be a real confidence buster if you don't deal with it," he said.

What was going on today! Was I so transparent that everyone on the planet could read my mind? The thought that even Coach, who I totally trusted, could get inside my head so easily rattled me.

Coach chuckled at the expression that must have been on my face and put a steadying hand on my shoulder. "Dakota, this isn't my first rodeo. There are two things you have to understand about this situation. The first is that it's a position every person in this room wants to be in. All the guys who've already lost would give just about anything to be where you are. So this is a good problem to have. It's a high-quality problem that you've earned the right to have, and that's a good thing.

"The second thing you should understand is that you're not the first person to ever experience this. Every competitor reaches this point. It's not a question of if. It's a question of when. Your "when" just happens to be right now."

"You're right Coach! Absolutely! I get it. I came here to compete. I came here to win and I still have a chance to win," I said trying to pump myself up.

Coach's eyebrows furrowed. "Did you hear the word you just used there? You said "chance" to win. That's not something you usually say. You always talk like winning is a done deal."

"You're right again Coach. I shouldn't have said that. I came here to win, and that's what I'm going to do."

"Slow down Dakota. I want you to win too. I believe you can win, but don't ignore the fact that your confidence has been challenged. If you ignore it, it's just going to pop into your head the next time you feel the pressure of someone else's skill. Your next opponent is going to be tough too. He might even be tougher than the guy you just beat—"

"Coach, I've got like ten minutes to pull this together, and right now you're not exactly helping," I blurted out, feeling the edges of panic threatening me.

"I know it sounds like that. But you've got this because your confidence is not based on winning. Your confidence is in your knowledge of the moves, and your ability to execute. It's in your ability to keep going and to keep moving forward regardless of what's happening. Most of these guys don't have that. They know how to wrestle, but that's all they know. They don't understand that competition doesn't have anything to do with the other guy. Competition is about what happens between your own ears. For you, right here, right now, your confidence is founded on the absolute truth that you prepared for this day to the absolute best of your ability. You've put in the work and the time. You're ready for this. You're ready for anything anybody throws at you.

"You came here with the confidence that you were bringing your best, and a commitment to doing your best. No one... and I mean no one can ever take that away from you. They can't take your preparation, or your desire, or your work away from you. Everything you take out there onto that mat with you is an asset you know you can trust. And yeah, you're getting a little banged up, but trust me, so is everybody else. I've seen your confidence grow a little bit more every time you've walked out onto that mat over these past few years. No one's been able to take it away from you because it isn't up for grabs. And today is no different. It's just another level to reach for. That's what competition is about. Reaching for the next level with everything you have." Coach held his hands palms up. "I guess the only question left to ask is... Are you confident in your ability to go out there and do everything you can in pursuit of that win?"

"Yes Coach!"

"Good," Coach said nodding his approval, "because that's all any man can ask of himself."

A Sprint to the Top

18.

A Sprint to the Top

"Your present circumstances don't determine where you can go; they merely determine where you start."

— Nido Qubein

Coach and I locked eyes the way I imagined warriors did just before a battle, and then I turned to face the spot where I would soon be facing my next opponent. Fifteen other matches were going on, but my eyes were glued to the circle I'd soon be standing on, trying to let the words my coach had said sink in. Two words stood out for me, and were now circling round and round inside my mind—confidence and commitment. I focused on the word commitment. I knew what it meant. Coach Pat Riley said, *"There are only two options regarding commitment. You're either in or you're out. There's no such thing as life in-between."*

I was all the way in, and as soon as I started thinking about how committed I was to my goal, and about how strong all the work I'd done leading up to this point had made me, I started to feel better. I had everything I needed to enter this battle. I had everything I needed to win this battle. That truth was mine, and coach was right when he said that no one could take that away from me. I'd done the work. I'd done more work to make extra sure that I was prepared to do battle today. I was proud of it too. I was thrilled to be here, and thrilled for this next opportunity to crush it.

And then I thought about confidence, and quickly knew that I had to push the memory of how close I'd been to losing as far away as I possibly could. Besides, I hadn't lost. I'd won. I'd won in a situation I hadn't prepared for, and that made it an even better win because I knew that if I could do it once, I could do it again. So even if my next opponent had moves I hadn't practiced, or maybe hadn't even seen before, I knew I could still win. Again, if I could do it once, I could do it again.

Granddaddy hadn't talked about anything like that, but I'd figured it out. When you face a fear that first time, you learn a lot about yourself. The first time mattered because that first time could turn into a life-long decider. In my last match, for the first time, I'd stared my biggest fear right in the face and successfully battled my way through it. That told me a lot about myself, and I could feel my confidence once again itching for another opportunity to prove how good of a wrestler I was. It also reminded me of how important it was for me to keep that goal right there in front of me so that I'd be prepared to do battle with any obstacle that got between me and my goal.

My goal was to win this next round. The obstacle standing between me and my goal was the Florida State Champion. And now that my head was back in the game, I headed down to the warm up area to get my blood pumping so I'd be 100% ready to do battle. The words "Carpe Diem" surged into my mind. Seize the day. Yes. That was what I was going to do. I was going to seize this day, win my match, and secure one of the biggest goals I have—a college scholarship. That scholarship was our ticket out. This win was Jenn's and my chance for a better life. I heard the PA system chirp to life and announce my match on mat 13. I was all business now, and purposely sprinted to my first All-American match.

My opponent, the Florida State Champ, stepped onto the mat across from me. In some ways, he reminded me of myself. It wasn't often that I met a physical equal in my weight class and age category, but this guy was as close a match as I'd ever encountered. He looked like a tough opponent too, and inwardly I could feel myself getting even more excited. I had good instincts about things like this, and already knew what my first move was going to be. This was going to be a good match—an epic battle between two teen titans!

Tweeeep!

I immediately shot in on his legs for a double-leg takedown move. I'm usually faster than most of my opponents, and I chose this move because of how easy it was to catch people off guard at the sound of the whistle. Nail this, and I'd be the one setting the tone for the match.

Unfortunately, he was ready for me and I failed to score on my first attempt. I gave myself a mental kick for forgetting that this guy was going to be good. No time for regrets though because I was feeling the pain of yet another vicious crossface counter. I quickly reminded myself that I had all the skills I needed to keep pushing him, and following a lightning-quick series of physical scrambles by both of us, we were once again facing each other. It was clear that neither one of us was interested in wasting precious time trying to size the other up, and we immediately attacked each other again.

We collided in the center of the mat, the sound of our chests crashing against one another echoing through the air. Now we were locked up in a collar tie hold. I heard myself breathing hard over the noise of the crowd, letting instinct and muscle memory guide my moves. We were both pushing, shoving, and pulling in an attempt to get inside control. I could hear my opponent breathing hard too, but he was staying with me while we traded moves, and I had to quickly push the thought that this guy might actually be stronger than me out of my mind. I had always been stronger than my opponents, and hadn't ever wrestled someone who could "manhandle" me. The last guy had been tough, but his build had been different, and in the end, it was my strength that had pulled me through.

Right now, it was beginning to feel like I was battling a version of myself—except that there was something about this guy. We were the same build, and obviously, both really great wrestlers, but something wasn't right... nothing was landing for me the way it was supposed to. He kept fighting for hand position and inside control, and I began to seriously wonder if he truly was stronger.

But that wasn't it either. He just wasn't responding the way I expected him to. His weight was wrong and there was something about his moves that didn't feel right. I wished I could call a time out so I could think and regroup, but yeah, that wasn't going to happen. To win, I had to stay in my head, focused on what I knew I could do, and then execute if I wanted to contr—.

Crap! You gotta be kidding me! He's a lefty? How did I miss that? How could I have missed that? Once I realized it, I could feel it everywhere with every move, his strength and movement all coming from the wrong direction. An alarm bell went off in my head reminding me that I'd only wrestled a few lefties. It was like fighting in a mirror—everything was the same except opposite. The good news was that I'd beaten every lefty I'd encountered. The not so good news was that I'd been a lot stronger than all of them, and I wasn't sure if that was the case here. This guy was strong as heck.

I immediately started to adjust. It wasn't easy, but at least I knew what the problem was. Knowing didn't stop me from giving myself another mental kick though. I'd taken too many things for granted today. I'd paid the price in my last match, and I was paying it right now too. This was my first big match in the All-American rounds and—.

Wham!

What the...? Mr. Florida had just nailed me with a lefty headlock throw that I had not seen coming. I couldn't feel the mat with my feet anymore because now I was the one flying through the not-so-friendly skies in a high-altitude arcing sweep. This was bad! This was very bad!

BAM! The sound of my body slamming onto the mat like a ton of bricks rang through my head. It hurt—a lot. Worse than that, I was flat on my back and now he was on top of me like a determined ton of bricks. He had me right where he wanted me, and I didn't have to second guess what he was going to do next, because if our positions had been reversed, I'd have moved in for the kill. Sure enough, he started tightening up his death grip, determined to squeeze the life out of me.

I couldn't breathe or see anything. I didn't know where I was on the mat and I couldn't quite figure out where my opponent was, except for the part of him that was smothering my face while simultaneously trying to drive my head right through the mat. He was pushing so hard it felt like it might pop! I didn't think I was pinned yet, but I was definitely trapped and beginning to doubt my ability to come up with a solution. I felt helpless, and strained to hear my coach's voice, but all I could hear was the blood rushing through my ears.

Not being able to breathe was always a bad thing. I needed oxygen to think, and without it, my head was starting to spin. I knew I needed to get out of this, but how? I was trying to grab hold of anything that could be used for leverage, like one of his legs, but nothing was within reach. Was that because he was a lefty? Maybe it was his position. Or maybe he just knew how to keep his legs away from me while he was smothering me with a headlock. With nothing to grab onto for leverage, I was just trying to do everything I could to keep my shoulder off the mat... hoping I didn't pass out.

I was frustrated too. I wasn't used to being in this vulnerable of a position. I was the one who put people in positions like this. Even when I first started wrestling, I don't ever remember a time when I was flat on my back being smothered to death like this. If I could have sighed, I would have because the list of things I was going to have to work on after today was getting longer by the second. Or maybe it was minutes. I wasn't sure because I still couldn't breathe and my thinking was definitely getting muddled because of it. But even that didn't stop the wave of reality that flooded me. I hadn't trained deep enough. I'd taken too much for granted, and now I was alone in my own little dark scary collapsing world. I refused to give up though. I wouldn't... I just wouldn't. That was all there was to it, and I started to search my body for any muscle I might be able to leverage into a move.

Tweeeep!

Was that the whistle? I thought I'd heard it, and then I knew I'd heard it because my opponent loosened his death grip and rolled off of me, and I was finally able to draw in a whole breath. I opened my eyes and saw him walking back the center of the mat. Was the match over I wondered. A wave of disbelief flooded over me as I sat up. Did I get pinned? I didn't think I'd heard the referee slap the mat, but I hadn't been able to hear or see anything.

I was starting to come back to my senses now, and was embarrassed to the core of my bones at how quickly and easily I'd lost. I was afraid to look towards my coach. I didn't want to see the look on his face, but I couldn't help myself. When I did, it took a few seconds for the words he was yelling to register.

"Get up! Come on Dakota! You got this! You can do this! Go!" he yelled.

I looked back at my opponent. He wasn't smiling. He was still standing in the center of the circle, which seemed a little further away than it should have been, and then I understood. I was out of bounds. The Florida Champ had thrown and pinned me in the out of bounds area. The pin didn't count! I hadn't lost! I was still in this!

I quickly pulled my thoughts together and walked back in the center of the circle ready to continue our battle. I was better prepared this time. I knew he was a lefty. I knew he was strong too. And I knew that I was going to have to outfox him. I needed to take away his momentum by setting the tone for how I wanted the rest of the match to go. And when it was done, he'd always remember me as the one who got away.

We were quickly into another hand fight. But this one was fake on my part. He didn't know it yet, but I was setting him up. To get the upper hand, I had to allow him to gain solid control of both of my hands. I was betting that he was used to being in charge of a match too, and that the false sense of control he would get from having secured my arms would have him believing that I was no longer a threat. It seemed like it was working because I could feel his body loosening up a little bit.

My plan was to quickly and unexpectedly drop my body level below his and then explode in towards his undefended legs for an armless double leg takedown move. If he's like every other human being, his instinct would be to protect himself from the fall by letting go of my arms. It was a dangerous maneuver for me if he didn't panic enough to let go. If he managed to keep his cool, then he'd have both of my arms pinned behind my back and I'd be the one in trouble. I was confident about this move though—I just had to hit it right, and then he'd have that falling feeling and release my wrists in order to break his own fall.

I moved, and it felt like it was working. A few moments ago, we'd been in a standing position, with him holding my wrists, leaning his body weight into me. His goal had been to fatigue my arms, but I simply took away that support and now I was in really deep on both his legs. My hard muscular shoulder was in his gut, but instead of falling backward the way I wanted him to, he folded in half over me.

Why wouldn't this guy cooperate! I'd done exactly what I wanted to do, but he was still holding onto my arms which were now securely pinned behind my back. It was not an ideal result. *Relax.... Don't panic...,* I told myself. I was still in very deep, and still in the perfect position for an armless double leg takedown. Could I do it without my arms? It wasn't something I'd ever practiced, but that didn't mean I couldn't do it. It was definitely uncharted territory though, and that thought had me wondering if this was uncharted territory for him too. If it was, then he might be wondering why I wasn't "cooperating" either. *Good,* I thought.

Another saying I'd heard played through my mind. "The surest way to be nothing is to do nothing. The surest way to be something is to do something." It reminded me that taking action was better than continuing to analyze the situation to death looking for the perfect answer—which might not even exist! The longer I waited, the greater the chance of my opponent taking control before I could.

Maybe this was my defining moment. Maybe this was the moment when I would prove to myself—and everybody else once and for all—that I was a true champion. The thought thrilled me. I was ready for this moment and proceeded to drive my right shoulder even harder into his gut. I slid my head off to my left side and started driving it up and into him, forcing both of us into a clockwise spiral. Next, I stepped up with my left outside leg and pushed hard off of it in the same clockwise spiraling direction that my head was already going, being careful to keep my head in tight on my opponent, acting almost like my arms would have so he wouldn't have any room to maneuver.

I was controlling him now, and the momentum I was building enabled my right knee to naturally come up off the mat. That allowed my right foot to pivot and land solidly on the mat, bringing me into a strong, low center of gravity, standing position on both feet. I quickly pivoted my right foot clockwise in a sharp tight semi-circle, and then my entire body was exploding in an upward ascending clockwise twister forcing my opponent's feet off the mat in an out-of-control spiraling, twisting, and whirling motion. He was airborne now, and it was his turn to fly the not-so-friendly skies. I'd done it! I'd caught him off guard and he finally had to release the vice-grip he had on my wrists to fight for his own survival. His arcing motion peaked, and now he was on his way to crashing and burning on the mat. His body hit the mat but he landed on his side rather than his back and immediately scrambled to the temporary safety of his belly, which made it impossible for me to finish the move the way I'd pictured it in my mind. So much for a quick and easy pin!

"Two! Takedown!" the referee yelled.

I'd scored first on a really tough opponent and finally felt like I was gaining control and setting the tone for our match—and it felt really good. Scoring first put me back into familiar territory, and now my confidence was fully back online. My next task was to use this momentum to keep him down, and start breaking him down both physically and mentally. But he was a good wrestler, and as hard as I tried to contain him, he kept wriggling until he finally managed to power his way out of my grip.

"One! Neutral!" the referee yelled.

The score was now 2-1, but I was still ahead, and without any hesitation, we attacked each other again, grabbing, pushing, pulling, shoving, spiraling, level-changing, hand fighting, and anything else we could think of in the heat of the battle raging between us. Somehow, he gained inside control with a left-sided underhook hold that left me in a slightly weaker position with my right arm draped over his in an overhook position hold. I wasn't happy with this upper and outer position because he had better inside control. On top of that, I was still struggling with everything being lefty-backwards and just plain awkward.

I quickly reminded myself that it was better to be proactive than reactive, and thought about taking a chance on an opposite side under-arm spin throw. My concern was that it was a lefty side move, and I wasn't anywhere near as strong or fluent going to my left as I was going to my right, but it was better than doing nothing. It was also a big move that would light up the skies with our bodies flying through the air again. If I could successfully strike this move, the crowd would light up too, and I had to admit that I loved that part of this sport. With everybody cheering my move, it would feel like I had the home team advantage, and all the momentum that goes along with it.

It was a complex and dangerous maneuver, but as the saying goes, "In for a penny, in for a pound," and I put all of my focus into the move. If he reacted quickly, he could stay tight at the initial launching and get in even closer as we were both in flight. If he accomplished that, he could throw a leg in, or wrap his leg around my leg and have a bit of a hold along with some leverage during our decent. Then, after we landed, it would be a scramble to see who would finally end up on top. But heck, that last move worked, so I was feeling like there wasn't anything that was going to keep me down.

I tightened my grip with my right overhooked arm hoping he didn't notice the added pressure, and brought my left foot back in a swinging motion, like a field goal kicker winding up to send the football soaring through the uprights. As I moved, I realized that even if he hadn't felt the pressure on his arm changing, there was no way he was going to miss what I was doing with my leg. It didn't matter because it was too late to turn back now anyway. This was a big sweeping move that would take advantage of the momentum and velocity generated by using both my left arm and left leg, and I was committed to hitting it with everything I had.

With my left foot fully cocked, I pulled the trigger by kicking it forward with all my might in its pre-determined flight pattern between our bodies. My left arm simultaneously fired up from underneath in an upward sickle-like arcing motion cutting between our bodies and up through his left armpit, wrapping over and grabbing the top of his left shoulder from the backside. While doing all of this, I simultaneously pivoted on my right foot in a sharp tight clockwise semi-circle, arching my back and looking hard over my right shoulder, like a diver hitting a twisting back flip off a high-diving board. There was a lot of momentum and power in this wild lifting whirl, and I almost smiled doubting that the Florida State Champ had ever enjoyed being at the mercy of this huge tornado-like toss.

Wait! What the—? As I was firing my foot and arm up, my momentum was abruptly halted. My left arm had made it through okay, but my opponent karate kicked my left leg, and hooked it in a way that I'd never seen anyone do before! His maneuver didn't allow my leg to successfully pass through the gap I'd so painstakingly created with all the arching and twisting I'd been doing. Instead, my left leg came to a brutal stop before it got off the runway. That didn't stop the rest of my body from taking off though. And now, without the help of my left leg, my body was becoming distorted and twisted in ways I didn't want to think about. We were both headed for the mat again, and once again, I was going to be the one in the crash and burn position.

I landed hard on my right shoulder, and heard a deafening pop on impact that was followed by a lightning bolt of pain that seared right through me. It felt like someone had just whacked me on the top of my shoulder bone with a sledge hammer. The pain was excruciating and making it hard for me to do anything. My opponent's killer instinct must have been triggered though because now his hulking atlas-like arms were cranking my injured shoulder with a brutal half nelson. This forced a gator-like death roll that left me in a deadly pinning combination on my back.

I couldn't do anything. My shoulder was useless, but it didn't matter because I couldn't think of anything beyond my own disbelief of what was happening. How did I go from my big throw to being injured, and then on my back being pinned, with my opponent once again squeezing the life out of me, determined to put me away for good?

Where was the referee? Couldn't he see that I was hurt? He had to have heard my shoulder pop. How could anybody have missed that? Why wasn't he stopping the match? I was trying to speak, but my face was smothered under my opponent's body and nobody could hear me, and I knew he wasn't going to let go until the referee slapped the mat because I wouldn't have. There was nothing I could do and I knew it.

This isn't fair, I kept thinking. *I'm hurt! Ref! You're supposed to stop the match when someone's hurt. You're not supposed to let this guy keep pounding on me when I'm injured!*

I could feel tears burning in my eyes. I wanted to believe they were there because of the pain, but a part of me knew it was more than that. Every second I was trapped under the "winner" was another second for what was really at stake here to sink in. This was not a simple "take some aspirin and put some ice on it" injury. This was a "you can stop thinking about that college scholarship" injury. My opponent's weight was still bearing down on me, but it was nothing compared to the weight of my whole world collapsing around me.

Slap! Tweeeep!

Finally, the Florida State Wrestling Champ released his death grip and rolled off me. My eyes were still closed, but I didn't have to think twice about where he was headed, or how he looked at that moment. I'd spent so much time dreaming about how this moment was going to look and feel, and was now drowning in the reality that it was unfolding for someone else instead. I opened my eyes and watched him step into the center of the small circle, and when he turned back in my direction, I recognized the expression on his face. It was a victorious "That's right! I'm the champ here!" look of pride and accomplishment.

I knew what I had to do. I had to get up and join the winner in the center circle for the handshake. That was what good sportsmanship was all about. It was who I was too! Slowly, I tried to maneuver myself to get up, but could barely move because of the pain in my shoulder. I was openly crying now, and the thought of someone else's hand being raised in victory had me feeling like I might be sick. Somewhere inside my head I was aware that I was crying in front of 15,000 screaming and cheering wrestling fans, but my ego had lost the battle of trying to remind me that tough guys never let anyone see them cry. It might have been different if I'd won. They'd all be cheering for me and these would be considered tears of joy. Instead, someone else was drinking in their admiration and appreciation for a job well done.

I finally stood and dragged my broken bent-over body to the small inner wrestling circle, suddenly wondering how the heck I was going to shake hands! My right arm was a completely useless dead weight hanging by my side. The referee signaled for us to shake hands, but there was no way my right hand was going to be able to meet his on its own. So I took as deep of a breath as the pain I was in allowed, straightened up my head and neck, stood a little more upright, and used my left hand to lift my right hand and offer it to the victor. He showed me some mercy by just holding it rather than shaking it. And then he asked me if I was okay.

His question surprised me. There was no way for me to know if he was really concerned or not, but it was nice that he asked. That's one of the things I've always loved about sports. Winning and losing weren't "personal." Winning and losing were results. I'd never really given it much thought—probably because my view was almost always from the winner's side. Today was very different though. Today, I hadn't just lost, I'd been beaten.

A Sprint to the Top

19.

Beaten

"There will be obstacles. There will be doubters. There will be mistakes. But with hard work, there are no limits."

— Michael Phelps

Now for the tough part, trying to keep it together long enough to get the heck off the floor. I turned my head slowly, looking for Coach. When I finally saw him, my body just turned and slowly headed in his direction. I was having trouble focusing my thoughts and I absently wondered if this was what people meant when they said, "He's in a state of shock."

Coach was clapping his hands and nodding his head at me, but I could tell by his tight-lipped smile that he was worried about me too. I wanted to smile back to let him know I was okay, but I couldn't. I always loved sharing my winning moment with Coach. It was like a soldier reporting back to a general, and it had become another one of my favorite end-of-match rituals. There was nothing good to report here though, so I stared down at the floor instead, wincing with every step, hoping the pain would explain the tears I couldn't seem to stop.

This was uncharted territory for both of us. I'd been brutally defeated, and my winning streak was over. I could no longer think of myself as "undefeated." But it was so much worse than that. Wrestling was my ticket out of the neighborhood I'd been dreaming of escaping. It was my ticket to a good college and an education that would give me a real chance to make something of myself.

I looked up to gauge my progress towards Coach and saw Jenn waiting at the top of the stairs that led down to the arena floor. Her face was white with worry, and I winced again, except that this time it wasn't from physical pain. It was from the overwhelming pain of realizing that all the things we'd planned on would never happen now because I'd failed to hold up my end. I'd lost, and now Jenn was going to pay the price too.

When I reached Coach, my goal had been to look him in the eye. I'd always been able to do it when I'd won, so I should do it now too. I looked at him and tried to say something, but nothing came out of my mouth. It didn't matter, Coach was all business.

"Let's get you to the trainer so he can take a look at that shoulder."

I nodded gratefully, looking forward to getting away. At the top of the stairs, I couldn't help but meet Jenn's eyes. "I'm sorry," I mouthed, the words barely a whisper as tears once again started rolling down my cheeks. I could see tears on her cheeks too as she shook her head.

"Are you okay?" she asked.

I didn't have an answer. Was I okay? I didn't even know.

Once again, Coach took over. "We're headed for the trainer. We'll probably be in there for a while though. After we figure out what's going on, I'll come out and let you know."

Jenn nodded her head, and I tried to give her a reassuring nod in return. There was no fooling her though. She knew me too well for that.

Spending time with the trainer wasn't something I had a lot of experience with. Coach knew this trainer though, and said I was in good hands. As I sat on the table, the trainer moved my shoulder around a bit, but not too much. When he was done his assessment, he gave us his opinion while carefully securing the ice packs he'd arranged on my shoulder with an ace bandage.

"The shoulder's been separated all right. You won't know how extensive the damage is until you see your own doctor, but it looks like there might be some ligament and tendon damage too, so don't wait to get this looked at. The sooner you figure out what the damage is, the better."

"How long do you think it will be before I can wrestle again?" I asked, praying he would say something positive.

He shrugged. "I don't know. That's something you'll have to ask your doctor." There was an awkward pause as he took off the gloves he'd been wearing and packed up his medical kit. "Okay then... I'll be back at the arena if you guys need me for anything else."

Coach shook the trainer's hand and watched the door shut behind him. "You'll be fine champ," Coach said, trying to rally my spirits. "These kinds of injuries happen to guys all the time. It takes some time and work, but they go on to wrestle again."

I eased myself off the table I'd been sitting on and slowly sat down on the bench so I could rest my back against the wall. Every movement was a painful reminder of how much had just changed. "Yeah... but it sounds like I'm probably gonna miss this up-coming wrestling season... my senior year," I said, staring straight ahead at nothing.

Coach was quiet, and when I turned my head to look at him, his expression was serious. His brows were furrowed together, and I could tell he was trying to figure out what to say. After another awkward pause he said, "You might be right." But then his expression changed. "But even if you can't get right back into it, you can keep working on what you can, and maybe be an assistant player-coach for the team. I could really use someone like you to help out with the team." Coach never did know the meaning of the word quit.

"Thanks," I said through a bark of laughter that had me

141

wincing. "Hey Coach," I said, clearing my throat. "I just need a couple of minutes alone if that's okay."

"Sure.... Sure Dakota... I'll go out and talk with Jenn and your mom... unless you'd rather talk to them."

I didn't have an answer, so I just shrugged, forgetting and remembering at the same moment not to do that again!

"Okay... See you in a while," Coach said, hesitating a few seconds before leaving.

I settled back against the wall as best as I could and closed my eyes, listening to the sound of his footsteps fade away until there was nothing but silence. For a moment, I thought I could hear the sound of the crowd cheering, but it might have been the roar of the silence closing in and around me too.

I was finally alone and so grateful because I couldn't have held everything I was feeling in for another second. It was the trainer's face that had done me in. He wasn't going to be the one to say it, but I could tell when he'd tried to move my shoulder that it was messed up—really messed up—and his look was like the last nail hammered into the coffin of my wrestling career.

Now came the gasps—gasps like the ones I'd heard the guy in the shower making the last time I'd been down here. I hadn't known what his meant, but I sure as heck knew what mine were about. I'd lost everything I'd built up in less than 10 minutes. Could life really change so much in so short a time? Apparently it could, because it just did.

What had I done wrong? I'd followed Granddaddy's advice. I'd done the things he'd told me to do. I'd planned well. I'd prepared. I'd focused. I'd done it all, and still failed. Was it all just a bunch of baloney? Or maybe I wasn't good enough or strong enough. Maybe Granddaddy, and the people like him who succeeded at whatever they tried to accomplish, all had something that I didn't. But if I didn't know what it was that they had... how would I ever be able to be as good?

Beaten

Now I was glad Granddaddy hadn't been there. Grateful he hadn't been in the stands to see me fail. It was a small comfort though, because I'd still failed him. I'd failed everybody, myself included. No scholarships, no college, no future. *Enough!* I screamed inside my head. I didn't know how to feel better, but somehow I had to shake myself out of this pity party because pretty soon I was going to have to stand up, walk out, and face Coach, Jenn, and my mom. The longer I sat, the harder it would be, and at this point I just wanted to get it over with. I opened my eyes and looked around the small room. There wasn't much to see, but there was a stack of towels on the bench next to me. I grabbed one and wiped my face dry, determined to stop feeling sorry for myself.

In my mind, I grabbed the first Granddaddy lesson that came to mind. CANDI, Constant And Never-ending Deliberate Improvement. It had been a big part of my life since that day in the park. I'd used it to shape my life. It had helped me get here. I wanted to believe I could use it again to come back from this injury and maybe even get back to the level I'd been at. Instead, my mind conjured up an image of me sitting in a canoe, my paddle floating away beyond my reach. It all still felt so unreal and I wondered if maybe I was just having a really bad dream because it seemed so impossible that this could actually be happening!

I heard the bam of the locker room door hitting the wall when someone pushed it open, and then groaned when I heard the sound of footsteps headed in my direction. I grabbed the towel and wiped my face again. I just needed a little more time. "Hey Coach," I called out. "I'll be out in a couple minutes." That should have done it. He should have said 'okay, see you in a few.' But the footsteps were still headed in my direction. Tap... Tap... Tap... Tap...

"Come on Coach. I'm fine. I'll be right out!" I yelled, embarrassed at the sting of yet another round of tears trying to take hold. Coach didn't respond, and his footsteps were getting louder the closer he got. Tap... Tap... Tap... Tap...

Fuming, I used the anger to end the tears and wiped at my face again, wondering what Coach's problem was. Couldn't he tell I just wanted to be left alone?

When the door opened, I was already trying to stand up, determined to just get it over with. I practically fell back down to the bench when I realized who'd been walking down the hall.

"Hey Dakota," the man in the blue ball cap started. "Now... I know you probably don't want any company right now, but I can tell you from experience that closing yourself off after something like this won't do you any favors."

"Granddaddy?" I asked, barely able to believe my own eyes. Or had I finally just lost it. "Is it really you?"

"Yup! It's me." Granddaddy said, pulling a chair over and turning it around so he could sit straddling it. "How's the shoulder? Is it separated?"

I just stared at him, realizing he was wearing the same cap and jacket he'd worn that day in the park. "Ah... yeah... we think so. That's what the trainer said," I said, my disbelief turning to profound relief at the sight of him. My forehead creased and my throat tightened up as I tried to continue talking. "It's really messed up though. I just don't know how bad yet."

"I thought it might be," Granddaddy said, rotating his own shoulder around and grimacing as if it hurt too. "So here's the thing Dakota. I don't have a lot of time right now. And the truth is that if things had gone differently, I wouldn't be here now. But after what happened, I knew there was a good chance you might be alone at some point, so I stuck around. Sure enough, everybody left, and here I am."

I wasn't sure how to feel about that. If I hadn't gotten hurt he wouldn't be here? Was this one of those "cloud with a silver lining" things? I met his eyes and the words inside of me escaped.

"I just don't know what to think. What am I supposed to do with the rest of my life now?" I asked, sucking in a breath before I could continue. "It's hard enough knowing that I've lost any chance for a scholarship and that I've let everybody down, but I've been an athlete my whole life. If I can't be an athlete anymore, then who am I? What am I going to do?"

Granddaddy nodded his head as if he understood exactly what I was talking about. "That's a lot of worry to be carrying around right now, but let me point out that you don't know what's going on with your shoulder yet. And you won't know until you see a doctor. Now, I'm not saying that the doctor is going to say everything will be fine and that you'll make a full recovery. I don't know what he's going to say, but neither do you. What I do know is that you've got a lot of emotion tied up with all this worrying, and none of it is going to change what's happened, or help you accomplish anything from this point forward."

I almost smiled. The truth of what he'd said was obvious once he'd said it, as usual. "Where've you been? I looked everywhere for you, but—"

"I know, and I'm sorry that I had to leave you in the dark," Granddaddy said sadly, his warm smile drifting away from his face. "But I'm pretty sure you figured out that if my death was faked, it was for a good reason. All I can do is confirm that it was for a good reason. But you need to know that the reason I decided to come in here to talk to you wasn't just because you lost. I wanted to come back here and tell you how proud I am of you."

That caught me by surprise. "Proud of me? But I lost. I got my ass kicked."

"Hey... I've been here all day. I saw you doing your fair share of "ass-kicking" too."

I chuckled a little because he was right about that.

"Back when we were talking in the park, we talked about plans, and how good planning and work can help us accomplish many things," he said, his expression turning serious. "But even then I knew there were pieces of that puzzle that weren't going to make sense to you until you experienced a loss of some sort. I know you lost your brother, but that's not the kind of loss I'm talking about. I'm talking about when you put your whole self into something and lose anyway. Look... as hard as you try, and as much as you focus your efforts and energy, you have to understand that sometimes things are just going to happen in spite of all your good intentions and hard work. BUT... and it's a big but here... you're still the one who gets to decide what happens next."

"But I don't know what to do next. My whole plan just blew up!"

"Okay, let's talk about that right now. Your plan was to go to college on a scholarship, right?"

I nodded. "Yeah. That way I could focus on studying and wrestling without having to work two jobs."

"Well, even with a scholarship, you'd still have to have good grades and decent test scores to get into college."

"I'm doing okay with that. My grades are fine, and I did okay on the SAT's too."

"So you can still go to college."

I nodded.

"The only question is where."

"The only question is money," I countered.

"So you don't have the money to go to a big college. But what about going part time to a community college?"

I thought about that, but it wasn't an inspiring thought. "I'd have to live at home to do that," I said looking at Granddaddy. "And I need to get out of that house."

Granddaddy nodded. "I can appreciate that.... I saw your mom was here today. It looks like things are going good between you and her."

"They are. She's been coming to my matches, and she and Jenn get along fine. Pops hasn't been doing much lately. He hurt his back in September and now he just sits around. He's still drinking, but he's not bothering us. It's like he's closed in on himself."

"So... if you had to stay home for a while after graduation, could you?"

I took a deep breath. "Maybe... probably," I said with a groan.

"Your shoulder's going to be out of commission for a while, but will you be going back to work once it's healed?"

"Of course," I answered as if it was a dumb question to ask.

"Is there stuff you can focus on while your shoulder's healing?"

I nodded, grasping where Granddaddy was headed with all his questions. "There is. I can get back to planning and figuring out what to do next, and come up with a new plan. This time though, I'm going to come up with a plan B too!" I added, my voice full of determination.

"Sounds good, but don't put your energy into thinking about plan B. If there's one lesson you should have learned by now, it's that you get what you plan for. So if you create a plan B, you're more likely to need a plan B. Come up with plan A, and stick to it. As long as you break your plan down into small enough pieces you can accomplish, you're going to have good results. Let plan B be any adaptations you have to make to your plan A as you go along."

"You're right," I said, hesitating for a few seconds before continuing. "Granddaddy, do you think I need to change my goals too?"

"That's for you to decide. I can't say one way or the other. Right now, you don't have enough information to make any decisions. Once you know more about how long it's going to take for your shoulder to recover, you'll be in a better position to make those decisions."

I was searching my mind for the right words, but there

weren't a lot of choices, and my eyes found the floor between us. "I'm scared Granddaddy. What if I screw up again?" I asked, totally aware of how small my voice sounded.

Granddaddy laughed. Not just a little bit either. It was practically a belly laugh! "Again?!" he managed to say, his eyes full of sparkle. "Dakota, there isn't a man or woman on the planet who hasn't screwed something important and meaningful up. It's what we do. We try, we screw up, we learn, and if we have a good head on our shoulders, we figure out how to do better the next time around. We accept that we don't know everything, and that we can't plan for everything. Even if we could, could you imagine how boring your life would be without challenges? It's the hurdles and challenges we clear that make us feel like we're on the right track and that we're capable of reaching even greater heights.

"It's overcoming those same challenges and hurdles that put young men like you in the position to become leaders too. Our world needs leaders we can count on Dakota, and people like me are watching for young men and women—like you and Jenn—to step up. Some will step up to be political and religious leaders, and so on. But it's not choosing politics or religion that will make them leaders. It's the quality of their beliefs and intent, and the honest investment of their time and energy into their chosen community that people will grow to trust.

"Some of those leaders will be content to be small fish in a small pond too, and I want you to understand that you can experience just as much joy, inspiration, and happiness for your accomplishments within the small pond as you might in a bigger pond. So don't measure your success by the size of the pond you end up in. Measure it by the number of lives you've touched for the better."

Once again Granddaddy was saying almost more than I could take in, but I understood it all the same. Maybe it was because something about it felt right down to the core of my bones. It felt good to know that there were leaders watching and waiting for us to take over the reins. It meant I wasn't alone.

"There's something else you'll want to think about after today too. You came into this tournament as physically prepared as you possibly could have, but it seems like you tied all your goals of a scholarship and college to something you didn't really have control over. I remember telling you that winning was a tough goal because you can never control your opponent. The only thing you can control is you."

"I remember that. But I don't think I tied my goals together. I just kept envisioning the outcome I wanted and followed the plan that would help me win."

"Then what part of your plan failed? You didn't achieve today's goal, so what could you have done differently to have secured the win?"

I tried to think of an answer, but I wasn't thinking too clearly and just shook my head. I would have shrugged too, but gratefully remembered that I couldn't.

"It's okay... that's a question you can think about later. I'll give you some groundwork for it though. When you sit down and start making plans—which if I know you, will be tomorrow—make sure your plan works in both directions. That means you should be able to plan it out forward, but it should also work if you look at it backwards too, like with getting a college education. You can come up with a new plan that starts tomorrow and ends with you holding a college degree in your hand. But this time, think about your plan from the perspective of holding the college degree in your hand and looking back over how you accomplished it. It's kind of like reverse engineering. You might come up with the exact same plan looking at it from both directions, but every time I've reverse engineered a plan, I've always found one or two things that helped make it even better.

"I tried to explain this to you in the park, but you weren't ready to hear it yet. The situation is different now. And when you go back over the plan you had, you're going to see the flaw. Your plan had a human being between you and your goal of winning—a human being who had the exact same goal as you did. Only one of you was ever going to win. And as much as you wanted it to be you, there was no way to guarantee that it was going to be you."

Was he right? I tried to think but I was tired, my shoulder was throbbing, and it was hard to know for sure. My brows furrowed though, because somewhere inside me I could feel the truth of it. Somewhere along the way I'd decided I was going to win, and that was that. I was just going to make it happen. I thought about the look on my last opponent's face when he'd asked me if I was okay, and knew without a doubt it had been a sincere question. I would have asked too.

"You've got plenty to think about now, but there's one more thing I want to say about the fear you're going to be dealing with over the next few days. Remember that fear is part of our ancient reflexes. That instinctual fear response evolved to keep us safe from danger. That instinctual fear isn't meant to keep us from achieving our goals and dreams, but that's exactly what it will do if you let it. The fear that does that is the—"

"False evidence appearing real," I said with a crooked smile.

"Right! That's why it's important to keep moving in the direction of your dreams. Don't let that false evidence get in your way. Have you ever heard someone say, 'Be careful what you wish for?'"

I nodded.

"That's a bunch of baloney. Be deliberate about what you wish for Dakota. Be deliberate about your dreams, and take deliberate steps towards them every day. Wishing is what people do when they don't feel like they have it within themselves to reach for what they really want. Or when they're so full of fear they can't even take one step forward. Can you remember that?"

Granddaddy asked.

"I can. I will. I'll work on it," I said trying to muster up some positive energy.

"Good. That's what I wanted to hear," Granddaddy said taking in a deep breath. "Okay kid. I don't want to say it, but I gotta get going."

I wanted to jump up and stop him, to ask him to stay. "But... Will I see you again?" I asked, my eyes trying to capture every detail while tears started to blur my vision.

Granddaddy went tight-lipped. "I wish I could say yes, but it's doubtful. I'm pretty deep into the work I'm doing, and it's going to be that way for an indefinite period of time. But listen, I'm always watching out for you Dakota. You're my grandson and I'm really proud of the man you're becoming. Remember that. And rest assured, I'll always be watching out for you in one way or another."

"But I need you around! I need your advice! I need to know that I can talk to you." I said, my voice rising, the pain in my shoulder increasing as I struggled to get to my feet.

Granddaddy took hold of my arm and helped me stand. "I know it feels like that right now, but trust me, you're doing fine. It really doesn't matter what you decide to do anyway. I've seen you using all that you've learned so far and how you still keep learning. You're leaps and bounds stronger in body, mind, and spirit than you were back in the park. Besides, having someone around to answer all your questions is not the way to keep growing and expanding. Each of us grows in steps and stages, and every man has to find and determine his own way. Today was a big step for you, and as long as you keep using the methods you've learned, and keep putting your sincere intentions and efforts into whatever you do, you're going to excel. You'll find ways to contribute to your community, and ways to help others accomplish their dreams and goals while you're accomplishing your own—like if you decide to take on the job of assistant player-coach for the wrestling team."

My eyes widened. Had he heard Coach say that? He couldn't have. He wasn't here.

"Anyway... You're going to do great Dakota. And by the way," Granddaddy said, resting a reassuring hand on my good shoulder, "No one can know I was here. You can't tell anyone."

"Seriously?" I said in disbelief.

"Seriously," Granddaddy said with a serious expression that broke into a smile. "Well, I know you're going to tell Jenn anyway, so I won't hold you to that. But very seriously, you cannot tell anyone else. Jenn can't either. I know I can trust you two to keep my secret. If I'd doubted it for even a second, I wouldn't be here."

"Yes sir. We can do that."

He gave one brisk quick nod in response. "Okay then. I love you Dakota."

I was stunned at the words. I'd never heard them from an adult before. Not once. Not from my mother, my father, or my brother. I'd only heard them from Jenn. I'd only ever said them to Jenn.

"I... I love you too Granddaddy," I said and then watched him turn and walk out the door. When it shut I called after him. "Hey Granddaddy! Thank You!" But I didn't hear a thing, not a word, not a footstep.

I looked around the small trainer's room trying to let it all sink in. Granddaddy had been here. I'd seen him and talked to him, and now I was ready to leave this room too. I reached down to the bench to grab the towel to give my face one more good wipe and stopped in mid reach, my eyes catching site of the blue ball cap that hadn't been there before. I didn't remember Granddaddy taking it off, or leaving it, but my heart leapt at the site of it. Now I was definitely ready to leave this place, ready for my next adventure in living to begin.